DESTINED TO LEAD?

ASEMANA
BOOKS

DESTINED TO LEAD?

A novel by
Hushang Dowlatabadi

Translated from the Persian
by Hadi Dowlatabadi

ASEMANA BOOKS

Toronto, Canada
First Edition
© 2025 by Asemana Books

ASEMANA BOOKS

Published by ASEMANA BOOKS

ISBN: 9781997503019

Book Design: Asemana Books

Cover design & artwork: Asemana Books

To find out more about our authors and books visit: www.asemanabooks.ca

ASEMANA
BOOKS

CONTENTS

Preface

The Shahnameh (book of kings) is an account of Iran's pre-historic *Shahs* (kings) and *pahlevans* (knights) and their epic adventures. These kings and their knights are as familiar to Farsi language readers as Robin Hood and Jack Sparrow are to those steeped in English folk tales. As with all legendary tales, they are a mixture of truth and fantasy. Often the line in-between is blurred and most key characters in the Shahnameh have fantastic adventures battling one another as well as supernatural beings called *deevs* (ogres).

K'Khosro's legendary exploits are a well-loved part of the Shahnameh. However, in this retelling of his story, there is a greater focus on how religious beliefs differed across the landscapes where the main characters lived and their saga unfolded. Iranians, unlike all neighbouring countries, were fatalist followers of Zurvan, a precursor to Zoroastrianism. Zurvanism has three key features: first, that there is no life after death; second, that every aspect of every living being's life is predestined; and third, that greed is the greatest sin. These religious tenets have unfamiliar implications:

Preface

- That individual intent is irrelevant, all creatures live fated lives with outcomes already "recorded" in the *ketab-e taghdir* (book of destiny).
- That individual wants are to be eschewed, the book of destiny defines each individual's *ghesmat* (*allotment*) in life.
- That their leaders enjoy *farr-e-izadi* (divine blessing) which gives them extraordinary powers to overcome supernatural challenges and enjoy public adoration. An additional benefit of being blessed with *farr-e-izadi* is the ability to see into the future. Given the dynastic succession for shahs of Iran, *farr-e-izadi* also followed royal bloodlines. Remaining a blessed leader was conditional. If a shah failed to work towards the welfare of his subjects, he would lose the support of *farr-e-izadi*. This in turn would lead to loss of popularity and an incapacity to overcome extraordinary challenges.

This book builds on the life of a well-loved king from Shahnameh, K'Khosro, whose parents came from Iran and Touran and different belief systems. K'Khosro's story is used as a vehicle to explore the tensions between fate, expectations and free will.

The remainder of this preface offers short backgrounds on key figures that appear in this book.

K'Kavoos – our story begins during the reign of this shah of the Kiani dynasty, he was a jealous and vindictive monarch who did not act in the best interest of the people. Towards the end of his reign, *farr-e-izadi* parted company with him and he was profoundly unpopular.

Siavosh – was the oldest son of K'Kavoos. He was, by all accounts, an exceptional warrior and wise beyond his age. He was handsome and charismatic and devoted to Iran and to the welfare of her people. Siavosh was tutored by Zaal in matters of philosophy. He was trained by Rostam in combat and military strategy. One of the most famous ordeals suffered by Siavosh involves Sudabeh, wife of K'Kavoos. Reportedly, she was one of the most beautiful women alive. She tried and failed to seduce Siavosh. This infuriated her and prompted her to seek revenge by fabricating a tale of having to rebuff unwanted attention from Siavosh. The jealous king did not believe his son's protestations. Siavosh offered to prove his innocence in trial by fire –

which he passed proving fealty to his father and innocence in the accusation raised by Sudabeh. The site of this trial by fire is near *Abar-kooh* (the capital of Iran at the time) and named *Tappeh-Sukhteh* (burnt mound).

Siavosh lost his father's trust again when after defeating Afrasiab instead of putting him to the sword, he proposed peace and war reparations to avoid further bloodshed. Upon hearing this, K'Kavoos accused Siavosh of collusion with Afrasiab with the aim of ascending to the throne. This forced Siavosh to leave Iran and seek refuge in Touran from the vanquished Afrasiab. Siavosh then succeeded in bringing prosperity to Siavosh-Gerd, a far-flung town in Touran and growing popular because of his good deeds and nature.

Afrasiab – was the king of Touran, having earlier also ruled over Iran after killing Shah Nowzar. Afrasiab was sadistic and paranoid. He left death and destruction in his wake in Iran and Touran. One of Afrasiab's daughters, Farigees, fell in love with and married Siavosh. Jealousy and insecurity led Afrasiab to order Siavosh be killed.

Piran – was Afrasiab's senior military leader and advisor. Wise and measured in his actions, he appreciated Siavosh as a fair-minded but capable adversary and eventually came to love him. His interventions led to Farigees and K'Khosro surviving the wrath of Afrasiab and for the story of their lives to become part of the lore of ancient Iran.

Rostam – was ancient Iran's greatest warrior and strategist. He was a huge person and without parallel in hand-to-hand combat. He defeated or killed almost everyone who took to the arena against him. Rostam and his horse Rakhsh are ever present in the stories that every Iranian child hears about ancient times.

Zaal – was Rostam's father. Zaal, was albino and because of his white hair and red eyes many feared him to be a personification of *Ahriman* (the devil) at birth. Zaal was left to die in the foothills of Alborz mountains. Unexpectedly, Zaal was raised by *Simorgh* (the phoenix) who taught him how to be more observant and strive to understand any problem from multiple perspectives. Throughout his life, Zaal suffered from jealousy and mistrust by those who judged him by his appearance. But Zaal's own thirst for knowledge and Simorgh's teachings made him one of the wisest men of any era.

DESTINED TO LEAD?

Chapter 1: From Ghalla

to Siavosh-Gerd

He was thirteen. Until a few days earlier, he had lived in a one room hut in Ghalla. His loving parents were Chehra and Nozeh. His days had been filled with chores at home and in looking after the sheep. Once his chores were done, he loved to practice shooting with his bow and arrow and ride horses. Now, he was sitting in a splendid villa. He had been told that his real parents were Siavosh and Farigees – not shepherd and shepherdess, but the crown prince of Iran and a princess from Touran. That he had been placed in foster care to keep him safe. Because his grandparents K'Kavoos, the king of Iran and Afrasiab, the king of Touran were sworn blood-enemies and suspicious of anyone or anything that could take away their kingdom. To top it all, his name was not Little-man, as he was called by his foster parents, but K'Khosro and he was destined to become ruler of Iran.

K'Khosro had just begun to learn about his dead father. Siavosh was fondly remembered for being: considerate, courageous and wise. Trained in the martial arts and military leadership by Rostam and in philosophy by Zaal, he had been expected to lead Iran into a new golden age. Siavosh had also been handsome and charismatic. This had landed him in trouble.

His father's young and irresistibly beautiful wife, Sudabeh, had made advances that he had politely parried. This had infuriated Sudabeh whose advances had never been rejected. In retaliation, she had accused Siavosh of having tried to seduce her. K'Kavoos, beguiled by Sudabeh, had chosen to believe his wife's accusations. Siavosh had lost his father's trust and could only think of one way to prove his innocence and not be killed or banished from Iran. He had suggested trial by fire to prove his fealty and innocence to the Shah. K'Kavoos had agreed and Siavosh had constructed the largest fire anyone had seen a short ride from the capital. He had then set fire to the enormous pyre and ridden his trusty horse, Shabrang, through it unscathed. The mound of ashes was a reminder of that dark time and known as Tappeh-Sukhteh. It was still visited by many who admired and loved Siavosh. Upon seeing his son's miraculous passage through the fire, K'Kavoos had made peace with his son.

Not long after this Afrasiab invaded northeastern Iran. K'Kavoos sent Siavosh to drive away the invaders and exact revenge on Afrasiab. Siavosh and his forces defeated Afrasiab and there was no doubt that the Iranians would slay them all if they continued to fight. Siavosh however, was not vengeful by nature. Wanting to avoid further bloodshed and deplete Afrasiab's capacity to attack Iran again, Siavosh decided to offer a conditional truce to the invaders.

Siavosh demanded that the invaders: lay down their arms, pay heavy war reparations from the coffers of Touran and leave behind three hundred of their finest riders as hostages. Afrasiab had agreed and was about to comply. Meanwhile, the news of victory and conditions of truce had reached the capital -- Abar-Kooh. K'Kavoos was furious with Siavosh. He was a vengeful ruler and had ordered the invading army be slain to the last man and Afrasiab's head brought back to the capitol. So, once again, Siavosh had lost his father's confidence. K'Kavoos, who was paranoid about losing his throne, thought Siavosh had spared Afrasiab's life to gain his support in toppling him and ascending to the throne in Iran. So, he sent orders to strip his son of his command and replaced him with Tous as Commander-in-Chief of the Iranian forces.

Dismayed by his father's reaction, Siavosh kept his pledge of peace with Afrasiab, released the hostages and asked for safe passage through Touran so that he could live in peace far from his father's reach and wrath. Afrasiab and his chief minister Piran had come to respect and admire the young prince's skill at war and his willingness to seek peace instead of revenge. They granted refuge to Siavosh.

Initially, Piran hosted Siavosh in his own villa. There, the young prince fell in love with and married Piran's daughter Jarireh who gave birth to his son Forood. Later, at Piran's suggestion, Afrasiab gave the hand of his own daughter, Princess Farigees, in marriage to Siavosh. The two were then gifted rule over a far-flung and impoverished province in northern Touran.

Siavosh and Farigees established Siavosh-Gerd and invested their energy and riches to bring prosperity to all who lived and worked in the region. The province prospered and soon had a mighty fort and bountiful farms and orchards. The people of that region came to love and admire Siavosh, despite his roots. This popularity alarmed Afrasiab's brother Garsivaz, who feared that Siavosh may displace him as the successor to Afrasiab.

No good deed by Siavosh would ever go unpunished. The prosperity of Siavosh-Gerd and his rising popularity was used by Garsivaz to fan the flames of jealousy and insecurity in Afrasiab. In time, he came to believe that Siavosh had been in cahoots with K'Kavoos all along and taking refuge was just a ruse. Siavosh was going to attack from within by appealing to a populace fed up with him as ruler. Afrasiab convinced himself that Father and son had been planning to rule over Iran and Touran together. Despite Piran's protests, Afrasiab ordered the death of Siavosh and ordered Princess Farigees confined to Siavosh-Gerd.

Some of the ill winds that had plagued Siavosh's life can be laid at the strange dreams that had preoccupied K'Kavoos and later Afrasiab. Both leaders were constantly worried about their stranglehold on power. Each had accepted the interpretation of these dreams, in the context of Siavosh's popularity, to mean that he was a threat to their rule. These unfounded suspicions led to Siavosh's exile and death.

In Afrasiab's case, his dreams led him to plan the elimination of Siavosh's bloodline. However, K'Khosro's young life was spared through the wise and repeated interventions of Piran. Piran had come to respect and love Siavosh in the field of battle and in keeping his oath of peace despite K'Kavoos' wrath. He had intervened with Afrasiab to give Siavosh asylum in Touran and was now crestfallen for having failed to save Siavosh's life in the face of Garsivaz' conspiracy theories. So, he pleaded with Afrasiab to let Farigees, who was pregnant, live in Piran's own compound. He further promised that should the newborn be a boy he would be sent away to grow up far away among shepherds without ever learning of his lineage, thus posing no risk to the throne.

As it happened, Farigees gave birth to a healthy baby boy and so it was that Piran put on a disguise and headed to northeastern Touran and the foothills of Ghalla. There, he found a barren couple only too keen to adopt a boy and raise him in the modest ways of shepherds. This was how the young man had come to know Nozeh & Chehra as his parents. But, unbeknownst to Piran, the adoptive couple were far from ordinary shepherds. They had been land-owners in Nimrooz and escaped to Ghalla after the devastation and bloodshed of Derangestan. In Ghalla they hoped to put the tragedy of their lost homeland behind and live in peace.

Chehra was thirty-seven and Nozeh was forty-four. They had been married for nineteen years and would have loved to have a house full of children. But they had learned to accept the ups and downs of life and instead of longing for what they didn't have, to be content with what they did have. So, when a rider, who despite his disguise was clearly a person of power and means, brought them a basket containing a bright-eyed baby boy and some silver coins to help with his keep, they thanked the heavens for their good fortune and took up parenting as ducklings take to water.

The boy grew fast, faster than Chehra and Nozeh could imagine. He seemed to be in a race to be older than his age; he was walking before he was 6 months old. At home, Chehra and Nozeh spoke in their mother tongue of Iranian. The boy started parroting them at an early age. And so it was that Chehra and Nozeh came to call the boy Little-man. The neighbours, on the other hand, could see a big boy with a halting command of their native tongue. He was reluctant to speak in company. So, they came to think of him as slow and mentally underdeveloped.

Little-man, like all children, modeled his actions after his parents. He saw Chehra spreading feed for the sheep, so as soon as he was steady on his feet, he would grab small handfuls of hay and copy his mother. Not long after, watching Chehra milk the sheep, he pleaded with her to teach him how to do that. After some trial and error and being kicked by an ewe or two, he came to be an expert at milking sheep and Chehra assigned him a few to milk daily.

While the life of shepherds is work and then even more work, there were times for play also. Chehra made K'Khosro a doll from old rags which they took on walks and made the subject of imagined adventures. At bedtime, Chehra would tell stories of good kings and their subjects. These heroes would endure untold hardship at the hands of deevs and other evil creatures, but eventually good would triumph over evil because they were wise, fair and brave.

Chehra, as a traditional woman of Nimrooz was a fatalist and her stories were in keeping with this belief. She firmly believed that every being's actions, from birth to death, was predetermined by the almighty. Nothing we could contemplate or do would lead to a deviation from our fated path in life. Even when choosing between two actions, the contemplation and doubt about which to select and the eventual selection have already been fated. This was too difficult a concept for Little-man to fully appreciate at his tender age. So Little-man's version of fatalism was that his mother and father were the ultimate forces determining whatever happened in his life. As he came to learn about everything being under the control of fate, he started forming the notion that perhaps fate was a bigger version of Nozeh or Chehra who could treat them like he did his ragdoll; taking people by the hand on whatever adventures they pleased. As he grew and heard Chehra and Nozeh discussing fate, he realized that Nozeh did not share in his wife's belief. So, thought Little-man, perhaps fate was a gigantic Chehra.

At seven, K'Khosro had grown so big that he asked Nozeh if he could assist him in taking the flock to pasture. He knew that this was no picnic and there would be no time for play or mid-day snacks of milk and honey. Yet, he knew that in his race to grow up fast, there was little else that could affirm his coming of age better than being seen to work alongside his father.

Shepherding was tough on Little-man. He had to run to keep up with Nozeh's long strides and Nozeh was a man of few words. So, instead of chatting with Chehra all day, he came to be more observant of the world around him and take time to contemplate what he could see.

Seeing the many wild animals in the wild sparked Little-man's interest to hunt. Nozeh, who abhorred the idea of taking any life, tried to interest Little-man in simply enjoying the beauty in nature and dissuade him from taking up hunting. But he failed. Little-man made himself a bow from an oak sapling and some dried sheep-gut. He made arrows from short straight branches of poplar and started practicing by shooting at boulders and tree-trunks as an imagined game. He grew more competent and couldn't contain his joy whenever he managed to hit his targets. However, the very first time his arrow found a rabbit, he was overwhelmed by a flood of unfamiliar emotions. It was not joy or sadness. It was not pride or shame. He stood motionless as the rabbit struggled to hold on to life for a short while and then lay still. At that point Little-man realized that all he wished was for the rabbit to bounce up and disappear in the undergrowth. He even thought about animating the rabbit himself, as he often did with his rag-doll, but he knew that nothing he could do would bring the rabbit back to life. He took the rabbit to Nozeh, who could not hide his woe and disappointment. Gloom cast a dark shadow on their return from pasture that day.

Little-man was convinced that he should break his bow and forsake hunting forever.

When they returned from pasture, Little-man saw the other side of his adventure. Chehra was overjoyed at seeing the rabbit and could not stop praising Little-man for bringing home their dinner. Meanwhile, Nozeh refused to share in the feast of grilled rabbit prepared by Chehra, turning to water and bread for his supper. Chehra said, your father is refusing to eat rabbit because he is opposed to taking an innocent life. I, on the other hand, believe it was the rabbit's fate to be your prey. There is nothing more powerful than the hand of destiny. If the rabbit was not fated to be our meal tonight, it would never have been born; it would not have hopped into your field of view; and your arrow would have missed its target. At hearing this explanation Little-man felt less awkward at having taken the rabbit, but he could not ignore the furrowed brow of his father.

The next day, as Little-man joined Nozeh on the trek to pasture, he didn't take his bow and arrow. Nozeh noticed this as they were leaving their hut and surprised him by saying it would be wise to bring his bow. He said, "The wilderness is full of possible dangers and men need to be able to defend what is theirs." Little-man only heard one word of that sentence – *men*. He had arrived! He made a show of picking up his bow & arrows and assumed the role of the defender for their herd.   During that day, Nozeh spoke about the difference between shedding blood needlessly and in defence of one's life, livelihood and beliefs. He didn't contradict Chehra directly, but posed an alternative view for Little-man to consider. He said how could one ever test a belief that asserts "everything that happens in their life is predetermined"? How could they be free of the circular argument that their decision to do something was not something that was pre-determined along with the outcome of that decision? And to encourage Little-man in continuing to improve his skill at archery, he built a stronger bow – setting aside the question of whether this was for self-defence or hunting.

Three years passed during which Little-man grew stronger, learned how to ride, care for horses and excel at archery. At ten, he was physically as well developed and as skillful as young men twice his age. His accomplishments were a source of pride for his parents, but they also lived each day and new accomplishment with growing trepidation. They knew the time would soon come when the stranger who delivered them their pride and joy would return and take their son away. Little-man himself was like other adolescent boys. He saw himself as a strong and skillful young man keen to see and experience the world beyond Ghalla.

He was no longer satisfied with hunting rabbit and deer. Chehra had been telling him stories about how champions had defeated *deevs*. He thought he should prepare for that ultimate battle by first hunting tigers and lions. Especially, as these were closer to what Nozeh accepted as appropriate action for a skilled bowman protecting his flock. Nozeh warned him to be careful and avoid the dangers of stalking such animals but Little-man felt he had found the right compromise between his love of hunting and the need to only shed blood in defence against predators. He was fearless, even when facing a big cat. Afterall, the champions in Chehra's tales of heroism had been successful without sustaining a scratch. He should be able to do the same. Furthermore, he would parrot Chehra saying "... that if he is fated to confront and vanquish a lion, it wouldn't do for him to avoid the lion as the lion would come hunting him to fulfill what had been pre-destined."

Piran had been visiting Ghalla once in a while, always in disguise and free from his entourage of riders. These mysterious visits had convinced the villagers that Piran was a person with special powers and able to see into the unknown. Soon after Little-man's tenth birthday, Piran visited Chehra and Nozeh to check on the boy. Afterall, he had promised Afrasiab to make sure the boy would never grow to threaten his throne. This time, Piran arrived with clothes for the boy and a spare horse. Having witnessed how quickly Little-man had developed to be a strong and skillful young man, Piran had foreseen that this time he would not be returning from Ghalla alone.

Little-man remembered the stranger's visits, year after year. He had trouble understanding why his parents would bow before their visitor and yet the stranger would be so kind and solicitous towards him. Why was he, a shepherd's son, deserving such special treatment? On this last visit, he was even more puzzled by the extra horse and saddle bag of clothes. Piran said that his parents have told him about his skill as a hunter and rider, and that he has come to take Little-man to where he can train to become a *pahlevan* (champion warrior) like those in Chehra's tales.

Piran said, "There is a lot more to being a *pahlevan* than expertise in riding and hunting and this is a very special opportunity." Nozeh added that while they had to stay behind to look after their flock, Little-man could come and visit his family anytime.

Parting was difficult. Chehra could not stop crying. Nozeh was tearing up. Chehra helped Little-man wash his face and put on his new clothes. But, his calloused hands and the dirt under his finger-nails spoke of a humble life not in keeping with his fine new clothes. Piran, tried to give some silver coins to Chehra and Nozeh, but Nozeh brought a full sack of coins and tied it to Little-man's saddle, saying" … we knew that someday you would be leaving us, and have saved the money we were given for your keep to help with your expenses when you leave home." And so it was that Little-man gathered the reins of the spare horse and stood next to Piran He was excited at the prospect of training to become a *pahlevan* but heart-broken to leave his family behind.

Piran rested his hand on Nozeh's shoulder as a sign of gratitude and respect. He turned and mounted his horse, in turn, Little-man jumped on his saddle in one motion demonstrating to Piran that he needed to learn a lot about becoming a *pahlevan*, but his skill as a rider may already be sufficiently advanced. Initially, Little-man rode alongside Piran. However, when they joined Piran's entourage, waiting out of sight of the village, he saw how the other riders bowed to Piran and rode behind him, and so he too followed suit and rode behind Piran.

They rode for three days before reaching a large city. This was a totally new experience for Little-man. The crowded streets, buildings that were cheek-by-jowl and the noise were all new to him. He then found himself entering through a pair of large gates into the sanctuary of a large quiet courtyard. The only sounds were their horses and a fountain splashing into a tiled pool surrounded by a formal garden. The courtyard was surrounded by magnificent buildings on each side. One building, the serai, was devoted to the noble women, their entourage and the children. Piran dismounted and invited Little-man to follow suit. He could see that the young man was both tired and lost in the new setting. Piran gently ushered him to the serai saying he would soon find his way around his new home.

The various residents of the compound from the footmen to the head of housekeeping were surprised at the presence of their new guest. Except for Piran and his wife Golshahr none knew who he was nor spoke with him. Piran knew that this would not last long. Afrasiab had an extensive network of spies throughout the realm and news of the newcomer would soon reach him. His long rule was predicated by a ruthless elimination of any potential threats. Piran needed to bring this news to Afrasiab himself and to convince him that the young man posed no threat to the paranoid ruler.

Piran had a difficult task ahead that would, no doubt, introduce even greater upheaval into Little-man's young life. First, he needed to convince him that Nozeh and Chehra were his foster parents. Then, he needed to tell him that his father had been Siavosh, the crown prince of Iran, before taking refuge in Touran; that his mother was Farigees, the daughter of the Shah of Touran; and that his own name was not Little-man but K'Khosro. He needed to make sure K'Khosro does not learn that Afrasiab's suspicions had brought tragedy to his family. He also needed to make sure that no one in his own household would inform Afrasiab of K'Khosro's presence until he had prepared K'Khosro for that meeting.

Piran needed to convince K'Khosro that he had been a great friend of his parents and would do his utmost to be his protector. He knew that eventually, K'Khosro would learn of why his father was dead and his mother in exile. Yet, Piran needed to make sure that in learning about his family history, K'Khosro would not grow vengeful against Afrasiab. If he could succeed in that, he would also be true to his promise to Afrasiab that no one from Siavosh's bloodline would ever be a threat to him or his throne. So began laying the groundwork for K'Khosro to learn about his family and the perilous journey ahead.

Late one night, Piran received a messenger summoning him to the court. Given the timing, Piran suspected that Afrasiab must have had a nightmare. He knew that Afrasiab would often react to a nightmare with cascading suspicious thoughts and vengeful acts. He was familiar with Afrasiab's hasty and, often, disastrous decision-making. Yet, he also knew that his own life was not in danger but feared for K'Khosro. He wondered if his success in saving K'Khosro from the executioner's blade at birth was only a thirteen-year reprieve.

When Piran arrived at the court, he was led to Afrasiab's bedchamber where the king was obviously in distress.

Ashen faced and still in his nightgown, he invited Piran to sit and began to tell him about his nightmare. Afrasiab said: "I have repeatedly dreamt that someone borne of royal blood would grow up to become a hideous monster swallowing the whole kingdom of Touran." Addressing Piran the distressed king said, "you are an expert on dreams and their interpretation. You know that a repeated nightmare cannot be ignored. I know of only one person who fits the prophecy -- K'Khosro! Didn't you promise to slay him at the slightest sign that he may pose a risk to me? Why are you protecting him?"

Piran replied that he has indeed kept his word and that K'Khosro, while of royal blood and a strong young man, is developmentally challenged and does not have the mental capacity to ever pose a risk to Afrasiab. He asked Afrasiab to interview K'Khosro and judge the young man's competency for himself. "If" Piran continued, "you find him to be any risk to you at all, I will put him to death with my own sword. If not, I would like you to pledge that he will be safe from future royal suspicions." Afrasiab was surprised at being asked to make a royal pledge. But he trusted Prian's wisdom. Furthermore, he was still regretful of his haste in taking the life of Siavosh. So, he agreed and invited Piran to bring K'Khosro to the palace so that he could test the boy's mental capacity first-hand. They agreed to have K'Khosro appear before the king the next morning.

At sunrise Piran prepared K'Khosro for interrogation by Afrasiab. He told the young man about the king's nightmares and implored him to intentionally misinterpret his questions. "If you convince the king that you are incompetent, you can save your life." He said, "give the most outlandish and inappropriate answers to any question the king asks you. That is how he can gain assurance that you do not pose any danger to his reign and are not the terrible monster of his nightmares."

Dressed in a princely tunic with a gilded belt, K'Khosro accompanied Piran to the court. Then, K'Khosro was ushered into the king's private chambers alone.

Upon seeing him, Afrasiab was struck by how much he looked like his fallen father and his heart began to race. After regaining his composure, he said: "I have been told that you are the son of a shepherd. What can you tell me about tending sheep in the pasture?"

K'Khosro answered: "There is little prey. And I am missing my bow and arrow."

Afrasiab asked: "Tell me about the sun, the stars and the moon."

K'Khosro answered: "They are like a flock of sheep. The moon and the stars meander about in the sky and the sun grazes alone."

Afrasiab asked: "What do you know about your parents?"

K'Khosro answered: "The lion does not attack the sheep-dog. It only has a taste for sheep."

After this conversation, Afrasiab snickered for a while and called for Piran to join them. He gleefully said: "I agree with you, the boy is not right in the head." Then, he promised to leave K'Khosro alone. He ordered K'Khosro be dispatched to Siavosh-Gerd where he could live in peace with his mother. On hearing this, Piran asked K'Khosro to bow to the king thanking him for his grace and ask for permission to leave his chamber. But K'Khosro remained upright and just stared at the king and his guardian. Piran asked Afrasiab to forgive the boy's rudeness. He tried to excuse the boy's misbehaviour saying that he has been awed by his majesty. At which, both Afrasiab and Piran burst into laughter at K'Khosro's oblivious and disrespectful manner.

On their way to Piran's villa, it took all of Piran's self-control to keep himself from jumping for joy having successfully engineered the reunion of mother and son. In addition to obtaining a royal oath that would assure their safety. Piran really wanted to hug K'Khosro and had to make do by whispering delight at his performance as they walked away from the Palace. Despite Piran's approval, the experience didn't sit well with K'Khosro. Nozeh had drilled into him that lying was among the greatest sins, and all he had done in the interview was to lie to and deceive Afrasiab. How can Piran be so happy with the outcome, when what he had done was so wrong?

Three weeks later K'Khosro began his journey north to Siavosh-Gerd. To continue his training, Piran gave him weapons and armour and they set off with a train of mules carrying the goods that any prince's household could not do without. Along the way, Piran patiently answered K'Khosro's endless questions except the questions about Siavosh and his death.

As the caravan approached Siavosh-Gerd, Piran's mood grew more somber. What he saw was more than he could bear. As they approached the province, he saw parched fields, barns in ruin and abandoned orchards. There was not a drop of water anywhere. The fort was in disrepair. These scenes brought back painful memories and regrets about how he had failed to save Siavosh and this province from the misdirected wrath of Afrasiab.

Piran was remembering how Siavosh had helped bring prosperity to this far-flung corner of Touran. Exiled by Afrasiab, he had helped plant trees, built houses and founded a community that was the envy of all Touran. Fifteen years later, all that was left was in wrack and ruin. Piran recalled that when he and Afrasiab came to visit the valley and its city and fortifications, the king had declared the province "heaven on earth" and honoured Siavosh by officially naming it Siavosh-Gerd.

Piran wanted to stay for a long time and witness the reunion of mother and son and to help provide whatever they needed for a comfortable life there. However, he found himself overwhelmed by the ruinous state of the valley and constant reminders of the loss of his friend Siavosh. He stayed for as long as he could bear.

Destined to Lead?

Just as he was preparing to depart, the clouds gathered in the sky and it began to rain. The clouds had been estranged from this region since Siavosh's death and it seemed that K'Khosro had brought them back.

Chapter 2: The Path of Siavosh

Farigees and K'Khosro's first meeting was more like
strangers being introduced at a formal gathering than a
reunion of mother and son. Farigees had imagined her
thirteen-year-old son in many ways, but none were of
what she saw before her – a brawny young man with the
physique of a *pahlevan* to be. This amazed her. But
what took her breath away was how much he resembled
his father Siavosh in mannerisms and presence. She
didn't know if she should take him in her arms as her
long-lost child, or greet him formally as a prince.
K'Khosro was similarly at sea. Piran had told him a great
deal about Farigees' devotion to Siavosh and the
hardships she had endured. Yet, when thinking about
his mother, K'Khosro could not fathom how this
delicate and fine-featured woman could have possibly
carried out the daily chores of the sturdy and ruddy-
faced Chehra.

It took more than a few days and less than a few months
for mother and child to grow close to one-another as
Farigees' instincts as a mother helped her find the way
to reconnect with her son. As they grew closer, Farigees
taught her son about Siavosh's life and ethos and
K'Khosro came to trust his mother's love and rely on her

as his confidant. Farigees told K'Khosro that his father had foreknowledge of his son's birth and furthermore, knew that he would not see his birth. It was as if Siavosh could peek at his own future in the pages of the Book of Destiny – detailing his fate. And so, he had left extensive instructions with Farigees about where K'Khosro could find his father's armour and when he should go to a nearby meadow where the wild mustangs roamed and call out for *Shabrang Behzad*, his father's faithful black stallion. But most important of all, he had left detailed instructions on how K'Khosro should develop the many skills that would give him the foundation to be a wise ruler of Iran, restoring the kingdom to its former glory.

Farigees was careful to remember all that Siavosh wanted passed on to their son. She needed to tell K'Khosro that most people of Iran believed that their rulers were blessed with *farr-e-izadi*. And this meant that their rulers would manifest foresight, wisdom and benevolence as befits their position of power. But how could she then talk about K'Kavoos, whose very actions were proof that he didn't have a virtuous bone in his body? How could she explain that while Siavosh had been an anointed prince and a paragon of virtue he had lost his homeland and life to malicious rumours spread by courtiers who traded in jealousy and hate? Even though Farigees was a relatively young widow, her tragic life had imbued her with the wisdom and experience of an elder. Yet, she could not solve the puzzle of how to reconcile these contradictions. If K'Khosro was to realize his father's prophecy of rising to become the ruler of Iran, he needed to understand the responsibilities, temptations and pitfalls that lay ahead. Farigees struggled with wanting her son to avenge those who had harmed Siavosh. And, she didn't want K'Khosro to rule through fear, suspicion and vengeance. She really wished Siavosh had given her the freedom to help K'Khosro grow into being a wise and compassionate ruler free from being anointed and ruled by fate.

Farigees clearly recalled Siavosh's reaction to learning that she was pregnant. A knowing smile spread across his face and he nodded saying, he already knew! Then he added that she would give birth to a boy who was fated to grow up and save Iran. Siavosh then added: "Sadly, I am not fated to see his birth and I will not be alive to help him develop the character and skills he needs for his burden of responsibility." Later, when he was called to Afrasiab's palace, he kissed Farigees' forehead, gently laid his hand on her belly and whispered, "I shall not be returning from this trip, but K'Khosro, our son, will accomplish what needs to happen... In the meantime, your lives will be in danger and you will suffer many hardships, but you will survive and eventually, a *pahlevan* from Iran will come to take you there."

Early on, Farigees had not placed much credibility in Siavosh's predictions. She interpreted Siavosh's last statements as his attempt to prepare mother and child for the hardships ahead with the promise of great rewards in the future. She did not believe in fate. But through time, she had to admit that Siavosh's premonitions had been accurate. Afrasiab had ordered him killed and she herself was only just saved from the executioner's blade through Piran's intervention. Given what had happened, she was doubting her earlier rejection of fate as an irresistible force. She wondered if leaders like Siavosh were indeed imbued with supernatural gifts and the ability to see into the future when the need arose; was this the difference between ordinary people and those chosen to rule over them? She had no answers for such questions, but knew in her heart of hearts, that *being chosen* was inconsistent with having foreknowledge that one was doomed and being *powerless to change* their own life's trajectory.

Farigees also knew that rulers and princes of Iran were followers of Zurvan - the god of Fate. This made it doubly difficult for Farigees to guide and instruct a potential ruler of Iran in beliefs that were at odds with her own. So, she tried to find some way to explain them to K'Khosro without being judgmental. Initially, she thought of fatalism as a form of self-imposed subjugation. Perhaps in times of hardship people would rather not have to make choices and would be happier with outcomes if they believed these to be the will of a higher being. In time, Farigees developed other lines of argument for her conversations with K'Khosro. For example, a king confident in having been anointed and blessed with a gilded page of remarkable achievements in the Book of Destiny could confidently undertake actions that mere mortals would never dare to imagine, let alone undertake. This confidence could be baseless, but conviction itself is a powerful force.

After much contemplation, Farigees realized that she was duty-bound to describe Siavosh's belief system and its genesis to K'Khosro, without bias or judgement, leaving him to make up his own mind. But Farigees also knew that this conversation would be more constructive if it could be delayed to when K'Khosro is older. She took solace that she could delay this difficult conversation for quite some time. Her son was only interested in riding, hunting and the martial arts. She hoped this would give her time to for the challenging discussions that were sure to follow.

This time of reconning arrived much faster than Farigees could imagine. The fourteen-year drought had begun with Siavosh's death. The rains had returned at the same time as K'Khosro's arrival, bringing new life to the parched plains of Siavosh-Gerd. The pastures were greening and rivers were in full flow. The people who had ascribed the drought and devastation of the province to Siavosh's death, now associated the heavenly bounty with K'Khosro's arrival. When in his presence, people would thank him for returning the rains and prosperity to the province. They openly wondered if he too might have been anointed by a higher power and benefit from a *divine blessing*. This puzzled K'Khosro, and as it persisted, he decided to ask his mother if she knew what the people meant. Initially, Farigees tried to downplay the matter, but K'Khosro himself recalled that Nozeh and Chehra would often discuss the nature of choice and fate. K'Khosro recalled that Chehra believed in the irresistible force of fate, while Nozeh believed that we are responsible for all that happens to us.

K'Khosro asked his mother: "So, is the notion of being anointed related to fatalism?"

Farigees, who was still hoping to postpone this discussion to a much later time, replied that there were two competing beliefs, those who like Chehra believe in Fate, also believe that specific individuals are anointed as leaders and live charmed lives. Others, like Nozeh believe our lives are what we make of them.

Farigees asked if Nozeh and Chehra ever argued about fate? K'Khosro thought for a while and recalled that while Chehra and Nozeh had always been kind and polite to one another, they had, on occasion, raised their voices in discussion of fate. But Chehra would soon try to make peace by offering Nozeh tea or treats. However, Nozeh would remain grumpy for a few days after such discussions. Farigees laughed saying: "Chehra could probably regain her equilibrium quickly because she believed that is what fate dictated, while poor Nozeh would take a few days to understand why they had argued in the first place." But it was clear from the way K'Khosro described their discussions that despite their differences, Chehra and Nozeh always respected one another's beliefs. Farigees added that, from her perspective, if others were similarly respectful of deeply held differences that didn't impact them, the world would be a great deal more peaceful.

K'Khosro, not only didn't understand what his mother meant, he was upset that she had said "poor Nozeh." He resolved not to return to this topic with his mother again. Yet, the conversation sparked an inner debate about how and why people form beliefs? Why is it that many believe in omnipotent beings? After a few days of struggling with these questions, his curiosity overwhelmed his resolve and he asked Farigees: "what is belief?"

Farigees hesitated for quite some time before answering: "it is very difficult to describe belief. Perhaps we can think of it as a sturdy walking stick people have come to rely on to negotiate their paths through life's hardships." K'Khosro thought for a while, but he still couldn't grasp the concept. So, he asked: "Are you telling me that Nozeh chose to live a less happy and more challenging life?" Farigees realizing that her explanation was leaving K'Khosro even more confused than before, tried a different approach. She said: "Trust in other human beings is the cornerstone of living peacefully in a society, and shared beliefs provide the framework for building trust across communities." No sooner had she said this that K'Khosro's face signalled even deeper confusion. So, Farigees decided the only approach she could adopt in answering these questions is to tell K'Khosro about his father's belief system.

Farigees knew that as mother and tutor, she needed to tread lightly and be as factual as possible. So, she drew from Siavosh's own life to provide a richer explanation of his belief system and how it impacted his actions. She said that Siavosh, like most Iranians, believed in Zurvan – the god of fortune and fate.

Zurvan's followers trace the world's creation to thousands of years in the past. Before then, there were no beings, earth, or heavens. Before then, there was no space or time. There was however, an entity of infinite extent that had always existed named Zurvan. Zurvan thought they deserved to be appreciated and worshiped. However, there was no one beside them and to be appreciated, they needed to create a world of worshippers. This promised to be a tedious task, so Zurvan decided to give birth to a son who would carry out the act of creating a world populated with creatures that would appreciate Zurvan's grandeur and bow their heads in obedience. Zurvan also decided that this first born would rule this world.

The task of creating the world was to be entrusted to Hormoz. Hormoz' passage through Zurvan would take a thousand years. During this lengthy period, Zurvan was contemplating the tasks that needed to be completed. Hormoz development was more than two-thirds complete, when Zurvan began to doubt the wisdom in this whole enterprise. The thought of abandoning the initial plan led to the formation of a second son by the name of Ahriman. Zurvan was quick in recognizing the presence of his second son. He could have halted his development but decided that he should treat his sons equally. Hormoz was a long way ahead of Ahriman in his development and once born as ruler of the world would deal with his brother at the appropriate time.

Ahriman, being aware that the first born would rule the world, decided he would not follow the long gestation path of Hormoz. So, at the same time as Hormoz was being born, Ahriman tore through Zurvan's body and appeared before his father at the same time as his brother, plunging Zurvan's plans into an unanticipated and challenging crisis.

Zurvan had promised rule over the world to his first born and felt obliged to give Hormoz and Ahriman joint rule over the world. Zurvan gifted Hormoz with the power to create all that is beautiful, good and constructive. Zurvan gifted Ahriman with the power to create all that is evil and destructive. To aid in their efforts, Hormoz was gifted with *Barsam* the green sapling that can help with the act of creation and Ahriman was gifted with *Aaz* the insatiable feeling of want. With this gift, Zurvan sealed Ahriman's fate, as nothing can survive the ravages of insatiable want.

Hormoz and Ahriman needed a stage on which to create their armies of beings and conduct their war for taking full control of the world. Zurvan prepared this arena by first setting aside a piece of their infinite being to form a finite universe with twelve divisions (the constellations). Second, Zurvan sliced a piece of their perpetual being to define an era lasting twelve thousand years. Finally, they wrote the *Book of Destiny* in which all events that would be occurring were written down. This would ensure that doubt and individual decisions could not derail the intended outcome. Zurvan wanted to never lose control again, so they wrote down every detail of the lives of every creature, good and evil, from their birth to their death in meticulous detail.

Farigees did not expect K'Khosro to form a deep understanding of this genesis story right away. She hoped that he would be encouraged to ask further questions and delve more deeply into the belief system of Iranians. But K'Khosro took little interest in the events of the distant past and only concerned himself with what the *Book of Destiny* may have in store for him. He was proud of how the people of Siavosh-Gerd associated the end of drought with his arrival and wondered what other glorious achievements were in his future? Through time however, he came to question the corollary. If his arrival had ended the drought, what had caused it in the first place? He put this question to Farigees, who was plunged into despair. Tears gathered at the corners of her eyes and she struggled to keep her composure. K'Khosro, oblivious to his mother's reaction, continued his questions by asking: "do you knew where to find the Book of Destiny? Who is its keeper? And, how can I access to it?"

The torrent of questions nudged Farigees out of her reverie. She wiped her eyes, put on a smile and invited K'Khosro to slow down and consider these questions one by one and at a deeper level. She said, remember, only some people believe in Zurvan, fatalism and the Book of Destiny. When we talk about the Book of

Destiny, it is only meaningful in the context of beliefs held by some people, not all. Also consider the question of why an all-powerful, all-knowing entity would ever need to write down the details of every instance in the lives of every living creature in a book at all? Surely, remembering all of these details would be a trifle for the omniscient mind of such an entity? If you accept this conjecture, the Book of Destiny is unlikely to have a physical form.

Now, imagine that against all odds, there is a book, access to the book would upend everyone's life. Let's start with your own life. My deepest wish is for you to eventually become the wise and compassionate king of Iran. You will never have the skills needed for such a task by idling away your days. You need to work hard for many years to learn the lessons in sympathy, diplomacy, oratory, tactics and strategy that are the foundations for such a position. If you knew, by looking through the Book of Destiny, that you would be king, would you be motivated to better yourself in preparation for such a heavy responsibility? Why wouldn't you while away the time in leisure and sloth until the day of your ascension? If you know that you are destined to achieve a goal, no matter what, why would you make any effort towards achieving it?

Farigees told K'Khosro to reflect on these ideas for a while before asking more questions. She said, most people don't want to think about these issues. They find it more comforting to accept their life experiences as having been fated. To make a choice, especially an important one, is very stressful. What if you make the wrong choice? What if this choice brings harm to a loved one? For the vast majority of people, it is much easier to accept a choice made for them by fate. Much easier to make your peace with a poor outcome compared to when it is the result of a bad decision. Belief in fate can lead to wildly imaginative stories – such as the idea that the return of the rains is because you have come to Siavosh-Gerd. Or that you and your father have divine blessing, what Iranians call *farr-e-izadi*. Whether it rains or not is a natural phenomenon. How then, could the start or end of a drought in this corner of Touran be related to the death of one person or the arrival of their son in Siavosh-Gerd? We should ask those who believe in such a narrative: "if the Book of Destiny calls for Siavosh to die, why bring about a drought that devastated all the people of Siavosh-Gerd? Why punish those who had nothing to do with his death?"

K'Khosro listened carefully to his mother's arguments and after a short pause whispered under his breath: "some of the people say other things too. They say that the son will avenge his father's death."

Farigees was devastated at hearing this. For thirteen years, her greatest fear was of how thoughts of revenge would poison their lives. She had often considered what she would do if given a chance to exact revenge on Afrasiab. Yes, he was her father. Yes, he had ordered the love of her life to be killed. Yes, he had separated her from her son for most of his young life. Yes, he was an abhorrent man. Yet, while she despised her father and had suffered deeply at his hand, she knew that if the occasion arose and she was handed a dagger, she would not be able to spill his blood. Now, a third person had entered the arena and he too could claim a right to avenging their losses at his hand. She was plunged into despair and lost for words.

K'Khosro continued: "I have only met Afrasiab once. Piran asked me to speak nonsense in answering his questions. So, I did. Do you know how he reacted? He snickered! How can a man delight at his grandson's mental frailty? Surely, this is proof enough that he is a monster. What do you think I should do? Should I spill his blood? It is what the people of Siavosh-Gerd tell me is written in the Book of Destiny for me." Farigees replied: "Let you and I agree that even if there is a Book of Destiny no mortal can access it. So, no one in Siavosh-Gerd can tell you what is written about you there. Perhaps you will then agree to take people's mutterings less seriously and be free to make your own decisions. People project their hopes and dreams from the realm of fantasy onto the real world. I don't know what solace this brings, but it seems to help them cope with life's hardships. Their hopes have no bearing on whether, at some time in the future, you are the victor in a war with Afrasiab. Or that you avenge the many lives he has taken. These are matters that you will need to decide when the time comes. They are not predestined and they should not occupy your thoughts now."

Farigees continued: "If you become the Shah of Iran, you will eventually face Afrasiab in battle. He hates Iran and Iranians with every fiber of his being. I am sure that, should the opportunity present itself, he will not hesitate to kill you. What I would wish for, is that if you contemplate taking his life, it will not be to avenge your father's death nor for his belittling and laughing at you when you met. I wish you to take his life in battle, in order to defend your own. Upon hearing this, K'Khosro was reminded of Nozeh's words when he first took up his bow and arrow.

Farigees continued: "In my view, no personal or private reason is sufficient to take another human's life. I assure you that even if Siavosh was standing here with us, he would urge you to eliminate personal revenge as a factor in how you interact with Afrasiab and others." K'Khosro interrupted asking: "How can you be sure what Siavosh would say?"

Farigees replied: "Your father was a devout fatalist. He believed that fate determined all outcomes in the world. He believed that it was wrong to assign blame to the individual for their evil acts. According to your father, Afrasiab did not choose to be blood-thirsty. His brother did not choose to be consumed by jealousy and hate. Individuals have no role in how they feel, act and what transpires during their lives. They are simply game pieces moved along a board as planned in the Book of Destiny by Zurvan. Afrasiab was only acting out what fate had dictated and to blame him and seek revenge on him was a fundamental misunderstanding of fatalism and how it controls us all. Siavosh would continue by recalling how he was completely in the hands of fate when dared to pass through fire to prove his innocence to his father K'Kavoos. He knew that fate would determine if he would survive to prove his fealty. And, when he took refuge in Touran he believed that fate had chosen this path for him to bring peace between the two perpetually warring nations."

K'Khosro was amazed. He asked: "Do you mean that he had no fear from burning in the pyre? Or that he would be killed by Afrasiab when he sought asylum?" Farigees replied: "I think fear only raises its head when people have to choose among many paths and are uncertain as to which is safe. However, when there is only one path ahead, there are no choices. The path is defined by Fate and there is no uncertainty as to how to proceed. Hence, there is nothing to fear. What will come, will come. K'Khosro thought for a while and finally said: "Fatalism makes life easy." Farigees laughed and replied: "It is so, but remember that it is difficult to truly believe in and surrender to fate. Most people are fatalists when the going is easy, but complain about their lot when the going gets tough."

Chapter 3: Geev's Arrival

For the next four years, K'Khosro and Farigees led a settled and uneventful life. The most pleasant times were when Farigees would tell K'Khosro about his father's exploits. Through these stories, K'Khosro learned about the pivotal role Rostam had played in training Siavosh in warfare and chivalry. He also learned about how Zaal, Rostam's father, had trained his mind and shaped his ethos. Through learning about Siavosh's life, K'Khosro developed a deep appreciation for these *pahlevans* from Zabolestan and wished he too had such exceptional mentors. Sadly, he had no mentors or friends in Siavosh-Gerd. He was well-known throughout the province. People recognized him and bowed their heads in respect. He was seen as the anointed young man who had brought back prosperity to the region. But, despite being popular, he was treated as if he was from a different stratum of society than those around him. He was even given a wide berth by youth of his own age when riding or hunting. He never met anyone who gave him the sense that they could be friends.

K'Khosro gradually grew to be comfortable on his own and spent a great deal of time riding and hunting. He was now a deft hand at bow-hunting and no creature could escape his arrow. But, remembering Nozeh's ethos of never taking a life needlessly, he set aside his bow and arrow and began developing his skill in using a lasso. This allowed him to capture or stun the prey and release them back to nature. When taking a break from hunting or riding, he would often sit by a stream in the hills and reminisce about his time with Chehra and Nozeh. He missed them terribly, but knew that Ghalla was far from Siavosh-Gerd and he was no longer sure they would treat him as before once they learned his true identity. These were depressing thoughts that he could only escape by remembering that his father had foretold the arrival of a pahlevan from Iran to help him and Farigees return to there. K'Khosro wondered, where is this man? When might he arrive? And, how am I to recognize him?

One day, while resting beside the stream, tired of riding and hunting all day, K'Khosro spied a dust cloud to the Southwest heading towards him. Soon, the rider could be seen more clearly. He was a giant of a man. K'Khosro was very brave, but this site, even at a distance, unnerved him. As the giant rode closer, K'Khosro could still not see his face. What he saw was bushy eyebrows, a sunburned nose and a fearsome beard that reached to his belt. K'Khosro grew even more anxious when he noticed that the rider had a firm grip on the hilt of his sword. When closer still, K'Khosro saw that the man's deep-set eyes were just as terrifying as his immense, muscle-bound frame. His eyes were searching for every detail in K'Khosro's appearance trying to pry loose his deepest secrets.

As soon as the rider was close enough to see K'Khosro's face clearly, he relaxed. He took his hand from his sword, jumped down from his horse and knelt before K'Khosro. He then gave thanks to the heavens, raised his head and said: "I am so grateful that my quest for the past seven years has finally born fruit." K'Khosro quickly realized that this must be the pahlevan his father had spoken of and asked his name. Geev replied: "I am Geev, son of Gudarz. My father sent me on a mission to find you and pave the way for your return to Iran."

K'Khosro invited Geev to stand and drew him into an embrace. Then he stood back and asked, but how did you know who I am? Geev replied, you are the spitting image of your father in his youth. His beautiful face and charismatic posture will never be forgotten by those who met him.

K'Khosro knew that the arrival of Geev would open up many new possibilities. None were as important to him than the many questions that Farigees had parried. These threatened to tumble out and betray how little he knew about Iran and Iranians. So, he wisely decided it would be better to ask about Geev's journey and through that gain enough background information to ask better questions. He turned to Geev and said, you spoke of a quest that has taken seven years. Tell me, what led to your quest in the first place? Geev replied that seven years ago, Soroush, the angel, visited my father Gudarz in his dream. He said: "I have great news. Siavosh's line continues, his son is growing up in Touran. He holds the solution to all the hardships and pain that has plagued our beloved homeland." The next morning, my father sent it to me and described his dream. I left for Touran before the day was out and have been searching for you ever since.

K'Khosro could not hide his surprise. He asked: "... and you undertook this quest on the basis of a dream?" Geev was visibly upset that the young man would be so dismissive of a message delivered by a heavenly messenger to his father. But instead of criticizing K'Khosro, he remembered how many times while facing unbearable hardships on this quest, he had wondered if Ahriman, disguised as Soroush, had appeared in his father's dream to send Geev on a fool's errand. These were times when he had questioned the very existence of K'Khosro. So, instead of admonishing K'Khosro he simply replied that Soroush was a holy messenger and the keeper of truths. And my father's words are more important to me than anything. And you can see for yourself that the dream has come true and I have been able to successfully carry out the first part of my mission.

K'Khosro who immediately sensed a tone of reproach in Geev's answer realized his mistake and added. Yes, my father had told my mother that a gallant pahlevan from Iran named Geev would come to take me to Iran. Please tell me more about your quest. These seven years must have been extremely trying.

Geev said: "The most difficult part was to learn how to live among the people of Touran. There is a deep hatred between our two peoples. Iranians have suffered a great deal at the hands of the blood-thirsty Afrasiab. Learning the language and ways of Touran so that I could live among them and search for you has been the greatest hardship. I was ashamed of speaking their tongue, but in these past seven years no one ever suspected that I am from Iran. The rest of my quest was a systematic search for you. I avoided towns and the busier routes. I would only ask about you and your whereabouts when I met a lone traveller away from hamlets and towns. Almost always, they would know nothing, but I could not let the news of my quest become known. So, without hesitation, I had to put each of these travellers to death."

K'Khosro was only now beginning to come to grips with the horrors that Geev had endured. He asked: "was there no other way of finding me?" Geev answered: "Regrettably this quest was the same as going to a war. In war, you either kill or get killed. I prefer the former to the latter." K'Khosro then asked what they were going to do next. Geev's reply was simple. We must go to Iran as soon as possible. I will camp here by the stream, so that my arrival is not noticed by the people of Siavosh-Gerd. You and Farigees should gather the essentials for travel and meet me here tomorrow at dawn, so that we can begin the journey home. I am sure that as soon as you and Farigees leave Siavosh-Gerd, Piran and Afrasiab's spies will sound the alarm and they will mobilize the cavalry to block our route back to the border.

K'Khosro hated the idea of leaving Geev to camp by the stream for the night. But he also knew that the man-mountain and his bushy beard would attract too much attention in Siavosh-Gerd and that the news of the stranger's presence would soon reach the capital. After some discussion, they agreed to a compromise. K'Khosro cut Geev's beard short with his dagger and they agreed to introduce him to the household staff as Nozeh's younger brother visiting from Ghalla. The final challenge was what to do with the mountain of hair where they sat. They could not leave it by the side of stream as it could give them away. So, Geev put the beard cuttings in his saddle bag and gradually dispersed it along their route back to Siavosh-Gerd.

While cutting Geev's beard, K'Khosro learned about the hardships that had befallen Iranians since Siavosh's exile. His departure from Iran had coincided with the start of a prolonged drought and there was widespread famine in much of the land. Then suddenly Geev's tone changed and he confessed that he needed proof that his quest has been successful. K'Khosro asked what was still left to do and Geev told him that he needed to see the young man's upper right arm. Geev explained: "The Kiani dynasty have a distinctive birthmark on their upper arm and if you are indeed the son of Siavosh you should too." K'Khosro was happy to slip his arm out of his tunic and show his birthmark to Geev. Then he asked Geev: "... and would you have put me to death if I didn't have this birthmark?" Geev smiled and said: "I was hoping it wouldn't come to that."

Geev and K'Khosro returned to Siavosh-Gerd without attracting much attention. Farigees was overjoyed at the sight of Geev and could not stop crying. Without concern about anyone hearing her, she spoke at length about how Siavosh had described Geev and that he would come to take them to Iran. Then, she quickly gathered herself and reminded the others that it was mid-afternoon and they should be moving as soon as possible as they would surely be put to death if news of their departure was to reach the capital.

Afrasiab had always been fearful of Siavosh's progeny taking away his kingdom and there was no better place to ambush and kill them than along one of the roads that led back to Iran. Before heading out however, they needed to visit a meadow nearby where at sunset, Siavosh's horse, Behzad would be waiting by a spring for K'Khosro to call him. With this, Farigees handed K'Khosro the saddle and bridle that his father had used and sent the two men on their new quest. Farigees reminded K'Khosro that Behzad would be among a herd of wild mustangs. That K'Khosro should show the saddle and bridle to Behzad first. Then call his name and approach it calmly, stroking his mane and gaining his trust before tacking up.

They rode to the remote meadow where Behzad roamed with the wild mustangs and K'Khosro carried out his mother's instructions to a Tee. However, Behzad disappeared in a flash as soon as K'Khosro mounted him. They rode so fast that Geev wondered if a deev had transformed itself into the shape of Behzad to fool and kidnap the young prince. He was about to give in to despair when rider and horse reappeared and they all headed back to Siavosh-Gerd.

Meanwhile, Farigees lifted a few paving stones in their private courtyard under which Siavosh had buried a few treasured objects set aside for this day. This included his weapons, his armour, along with some gold coins and gemstones. Once the riders returned Farigees was overcome by the sight of Behzad in her husband's livery and could not stop kissing the steed and crying uncontrollably. Once she regained her composure, she invited Geev to take whatever he wished from Siavosh's treasure. Geev only took the breastplate saying this is the most precious thing he can imagine carrying with him -- it would mean that Siavosh is always close to his heart. K'Khosro helped himself to his father's armory and they took some gold and gems to pay for necessities on their way back to Iran. The rest, was left in place and hidden again by Farigees. The three set off on their journey in the dark, the two men wearing their armour and Farigees a helmet to try and suggest to on-lookers that she too is a soldier.

The next morning, everyone in Siavosh-Gerd knew that Farigees and K'Khosro had left town. The news reached Piran two days later. This may seem like a great head-start for the fugitives, but in fact, their route back to Iran was taking them closer to Piran and he did not have to travel far to block their path. Piran was furious at the news, He mobilized a battalion, three hundred strong, led by Golbaad to look for and detain the fugitives. Golbaad's orders were to slay Farigees and anyone who was with them from Iran on the spot and to bring back K'Khosro in chains to be punished by Piran.

Giving the order was far easier than carrying it out. The cavalry did catch up with the fleeing party after an arduous chase, but Geev found a protected pass and singlehandedly killed a great many of them. Golbaad and a handful of surviving riders returned to Piran admitting their inadequacy in combat with Geev. The infuriated Piran gathered one thousand riders and headed towards the fleeing trio at speed.

Meanwhile, the fugitives had come to a small tributary of the Jayhoon. They realized that they now faced two perils, one from behind and one ahead. The mighty river marking the border between Touran and Iran was in full flood.

They crossed the small tributary immediately ahead, but how could they cross the main river? Exhausted, Geev and K'Khosro were resting while Farigees kept a lookout. Seeing the billowing dust cloud on the horizon to the east, she raised the alarm. It was clear that celebrating their escape from the grasp of Golbaad had been premature. A much larger number of riders were giving chase. K'Khosro wanted to stand with Geev and fight the pursuing army. But Geev refused. He said there is only one claimant to the throne whereas there are many pahlevans. He could not afford for the young prince to die in battle and the prince could easily find other pahlevans to fight by his side. So, Geev stayed behind while Farigees and K'Khosro fled the river's edge and hid behind a mound nearby.

Piran and his riders arrived on the eastern bank of the river to find Geev alone on the opposing bank. Furious and proud, Piran shouted across that he would behead Geev for his sins. Geev pretended to be fearful and as Piran advanced alone, he back-peddled away from the advancing general. When they were out of sight of the other bank, Geev used his lasso to pull Piran from his mount and hog-tied him. He then took Piran's helmet and ensign and returned to the river bank where the remaining riders could see their leader's livery and ensign. So, they thought that their enemy had been vanquished and rode across with their guard down. Once they arrived on the other side, Geev disposed of them one-by-one until the remaining riders realized this was a trap and fled. Meanwhile, Geev tied Piran to a horse and took him to Farigees and K'Khosro's hiding place. When they saw Piran, their protector, in such a state they pleaded with Geev to save his life. Geev said that he had promised to spill Piran's blood. But they told him that the only reason they were alive was because of Piran's many interventions. They were at an impasse until K'Khosro came up with a compromise. He said, why not make a small cut in his ear using your dagger? That would fulfill your promise to spill his blood and it would save Piran's life. And so it was that Piran survived capture by Geev. K'Khosro tied Piran's hands and Geev helped him onto his horse and put its reins in his hands. He was set free with the promise that he would only let Golshahr, his wife, untie his hands.

Geev and company resumed their journey until they reached the eastern shore of the main branch of Jayhoon. The river was a roiling cacophony of crashing waves as far as the eye could see, keen to carry downstream anything within reach. One look at it, and it was clear why many preferred to think of Jayhoon as a sea rather than a river. They found a ferry on the shore. The smug ferryman knew that under those conditions any sane person would pay whatever he asked in exchange for passage across the river. So, he asked for their armour as well as Farigees as his fee to ferry them across! Facing this impossible situation, Geev turned to K'Khosro and told him that his ancestor Fereydoun had crossed the Arvand River in full flood on his horse. That this was only possible because Fereydoun was an anointed king. You too are anointed. You can find the way to cross the river on your steed. Farigees and I will follow you. I am sure you will succeed. And even if Farigees and I fail to cross the river, we have fulfilled our duties. She has brought you into this world and I have brought you to Iran.

K'Khosro realized that they were out of options. He urged Behzad forward and they braved the raging river making their way across with great difficulty. A short distance behind them, Farigees and Geev followed their trajectory and successfully crossed the river. They were now on Iranian soil and close to its most easterly border-town of Zam.

Meanwhile, Afrasiab was riding towards Jayhoon, he was consumed with anger and raging against all around him. When he saw that his quarry had already crossed the river, he wanted to pursue and kill them on enemy territory. However, his entourage reminded him of the way Geev had seen away companies of three hundred and one thousand riders and persuaded him that they needed far larger numbers to mount a successful pursuit in Iran.

On the western bank of the river, news of the travellers from Touran preceded their arrival in Zam. The town's governor and nobility rode out to greet the road-weary travellers and welcomed them to their town with pageantry. The people of the city joined in with fanfare throughout the streets in the hope of catching a glimpse of the crown prince.

As soon as the nobility of Zam saw K'Khosro, they dismounted and kneeled before him. K'Khosro wanted to jump down and help them stand, but Geev grabbed his tunic and held him fast on his saddle. He whispered: you need to signal with your hand that they can rise. The nobility rose to their feet and the provincial governor came forward and began his welcome speech. He affirmed that if escape from the clutches of the blood-thirsty Afrasiab was not enough, crossing Jayhoon in full-flood was confirmation that K'Khosro had indeed been gifted with *farr-e-izadi*. He then reminded everyone about Fereydoun's crossing of the Arvand and how his long reign had brought peace and prosperity to Iran. The speech ended with the crowd wishing a long life full of success for the young prince and headed into town. The nobility and their guests paraded before the cheering public and ended their day of extreme adventures at the governor's mansion.

While the hosts were celebrating their guests, K'Khosro's first day on Iranian soil was far from a happy experience. He did not like people kneeling before him. He did not like having to remain in his saddle instead of standing with the greeting crowds. His misery was compounded when at dinner time, he saw that he was seated on his own. This was worse than his isolation in

Siavosh-Gerd. In Zam, no one was of a high enough status to sit with him – not even his mother. K'Khosro quickly came to realize that for the rest of his days, he could no longer be who he wanted to be. He had to be whomever Iranians expected him to be. It was his first realization that his destiny as king was a life sentence to constraints dictated by long-standing traditions, not the freedom to make choices from ever expanding opportunities.

After dinner, Geev came to his private tent, standing at attention and at some distance. His posture spoke of a new relationship. His face conveyed no emotions other than obedience and he was no longer barking instructions to his young charge. K'Khosro was a prince on this side of the river and Geev's role as tutor had been left behind on the other side of the Jayhoon river.

After Geev, the nobility and landowners came to visit with the young prince and each retold the story of how Siavosh's exile and death led to endless droughts, failing crops and misery for the once prosperous people of Iran. They continued saying that K'Kavoos is king of Iran in name only. That *farr-e-izadi* has abandoned him and his reign failed to bring any prosperity or security to Iran. Their narrative continued with: "Now that you are here and have demonstrated your miraculous abilities, as in crossing the river at full flood, we know that Iran's fortunes will turn around. And soon after, you will avenge the blood shed by the monster Afrasiab. As-long-as he is alive, Iran is in danger"

K'Khosro didn't know what he should make of this. He tried to appear attentive and kept his composure. When the formal part of the reception was over, K'Khosro turned to Geev and quietly asked to see his mother. But Geev said that would not be possible. Farigees was being looked after splendidly in a ceremony of her own in the *Serai.*

Eventually, the visitors left bowing and walking backwards in display of their subservience. K'Khosro was finally alone in his quarters. He took in his surroundings and wondered if the rest of his days would be the same; a constant stream of visitors standing on ceremony; full of speeches bereft of substance. He really wished he could have the council of his mother. But he also knew that as an adolescent young man he would no longer be allowed into the *Serai.*

So, all that was left was to sleep. He was so tired he could hardly keep his eyes open, but his quarters were lit by eight large torches that made the room as bright as day. He didn't know if he had permission to put them out. In a corner, he spied a partition that hid his bed. There he found silk sheets and covers and two more, thankfully dimmer, lanterns. These at least gave a chance for the night to express a faint presence. But still, he could not fall asleep.

K'Khosro's mind was abuzz with the day's events. He first relived the exchange with the ferryman. How could someone be so greedy as to want both their armour and Farigees in exchange for safe passage across the river? Then he turned to crossing the river on Behzad. It was the horse which had found the safe passage across the river. It was a trajectory that ensured a firm footing against the raging current and delivered them to the far bank. He knew that he had tried to steer a different path, fearful of the path that Behzad was taking. But his ride had steadfastly refused to yield to his commands. How can anyone attribute the miracle of crossing the Jayhoon in flood to him when it was the horse's experience and intuition that had saved them? How could everyone interpret the crossing of Jayhoon on horseback as evidence that he is favoured by the Almighty. He knew he did not deserve any credit. He had no prior knowledge of Fereydoun crossing the

Arvand, but he hoped that in his case, it was his ancestor who had been pivotal in safe passage across the raging river. In his case, it was all Behzad's doing.

Finally, he thought about all the visiting dignitaries who came to meet and greet him. He was very uncomfortable with their kneeling before him and even more uncomfortable that Geev had prevented him from acting according to his nature and dismounting to embrace them in thanks. He knew all about kneeling before royalty. He remembered how everyone knelt and bowed in Afrasiab's court. He knew that his refusal to bow before Afrasiab was a sign that he has a mental incapacity. This had upset him. But now that he was thinking back on the day's events, he realized that he did not know the court's etiquette and his natural tendencies may be at odds with what custom dictates. So, he resolved to have Geev by his side to make sure he observes the appropriate customs.

Chapter 4: The Prince in Shackles

The distant and insistent sound of a rooster's calls woke K'Khosro from a fitful sleep. He tried to remember where he was. It took him a while to realize he was in Zam. He stirred under the unfamiliar bedding. The gold candlesticks were draped in wax drippings from last night's candles. The torches in the reception area beyond his sleeping quarters were still burning. An elderly manservant noticed he was awake and brought him a large basin of water to wash. As soon as he had washed and dressed, a prince's breakfast awaited. The table was groaning under the weight of the foods and fruits. But it was again, much to his disappointment, it was a setting for one.

K'Khosro compared this to the ritual of his younger days. He would have had a good night's sleep. The rooster would be loud and nearby. Chehra would greet him with a broad smile and before he was finished making his bed, she would be listing his daily chores. There would be a modest breakfast for the three of them and off they would go. He wondered if, sometime in the future, having completed the dictates of his fate, he would once again be free to do as he pleased? If so, he really wished he could return to Ghalla to live the rest of his life with Chehra and Nozeh.

As soon as he finished his breakfast, Geev came in and stood to attention seeking permission to speak. K'Khosro thought this was his chance to ask Geev to arrange a meeting with Farigees. But Geev said: "Lady Farigees is well looked after and comfortable. More urgent matters must be dealt with and the prince should get ready for travel." This came as a surprise to K'Khosro who was clearly no longer in charge. Furthermore, he didn't know where they were travelling to. Was this going to be a daily pattern of life in Iran? A puppet on a string unaware of what lay ahead?

K'Khosro asked Geev what was the hurry? Geev replied that his mission would only be completed when he was safely delivered to central Iran. He added: "Afrasiab is like a wounded animal, he may have decided not to cross the river with his army yesterday, but he can easily send a band of assassins to kill or capture you while you are close to the border. The sooner we leave for Espahan the better. Gudarz, my father, is the governor of Espahan." Geev added that a messenger had already been dispatched to Espahan to bring news of our return to Iran and Gudarz should be the first senior statesman to greet the future king of Iran.

By mid-morning, a long column of riders snaked out of Zam, taking the route heading southwest. At the front, scouts were rushing ahead to set up a camp for lunch. They were followed by K'Khosro, Geev and the nobility of Zam, who were followed by Farigees and her lady companions. At the rear, some sixty riders provided security. About three hours after leaving Zam, they camped for lunch with three tables set for the prince, the regional nobility and the ladies. As at breakfast, the prince was condemned to eat alone. After lunch, there was the usual ceremonial pledges and plaudits. Then the local dignitaries took a knee and sought permission to return to Zam.

The trip to Espahan took ten days. Along the way, they came across many hamlets and herders guiding their animals to pasture. The forward scouts would have already alerted them to K'Khosro's entourage passing through. So they had gathered by the side of the road to see the young prince whose return held so much promise for their future prosperity. They were there out of curiosity and hope. They cheered loudly and offered gifts well beyond their means to the riders passing through. The travellers would set up camp twice a day. At lunch, their tents provided a place to eat and take shelter from the mid-day sun. At night, there would be additional tents for sleeping quarters. During their travels, K'Khosro gained a little more autonomy and managed to meet with Farigees in private on a couple of occasions. However, beyond that minor victory, his powers could only reach to the point of being able to put out the torches in his sleeping quarters. But just beyond the curtain marking his bedchamber the large torches continued to light the night.

On the tenth day, they saw a large dust cloud on the horizon from the southwest. Geev approached K'Khosro looking overjoyed. He brought news that they are going to be met by the nobility of Iran. About half a day's ride to Espahan, the two parties met. An older gentleman, Gudarz, was at the head of the delegation with dozens of noblemen lined up behind him. As they saw K'Khosro approach, they all dismounted and took a knee in a show of subservience. K'Khosro did not hesitate to jump off his own mount and embrace Gudarz, pulling him to his feet and kissing him on both cheeks.

Gudarz was so happy he was tongue-tied. All he could say was that his joy at meeting K'Khosro was equal to being with Siavosh again. Gudarz then went to Geev and embraced his son thanking him for bringing back the light that was going to end the darkness that had overshadowed Iran for so long. The other noblemen gathered around K'Khosro and Geev and showered them with attention and praised Geev for his service to Iran. No one was going to forget his seven-year ordeal in finding and returning the son of Siavosh to his homeland. All were convinced that this was going to be the start of a new era of prosperity and security. K'Khosro took all of this in and tried to commit to memory the many new names and faces who greeted him.

After their impromptu greeting, the caravan of riders set off for Espahan. K'Khosro and Gudarz rode together, Geev slightly behind them and the rest in tow. K'Khosro asked about his mother and was informed that the ladies had not waited at the meeting place and had gone ahead to Espahan, arriving there before the men. He wanted to meet up with his mother, but knew that Geev would give some excuse that this was impossible and decided to bide his time. They rode on and arrived at the Eastern gate of Espahan Just before dusk. The city was more magnificent than any he had seen before. Crowds had gathered along their route to the governor's palace and the trees and buildings were festooned with decorations in celebration of his arrival. When Geev was not watching over him like a hawk, the prince would sneak a smile and a wave in recognition of their enthusiastic greetings. Eventually, their company arrived at Gudarz' magnificent palace, on the northern shore of Zayande-rood.

They entered the Hall of The People. The floor was covered in fine silk carpets. Throw pillows and ottomans filled the space, except for a raised golden platform at the far end of the hall. Gudarz asked the prince to rest on the platform and K'Khosro took Gudarz' hand and they sat on the platform together. Before them, their entourage took their places, according to rank and age, around the hall. The more important sat near the platform and those of lower rank nearer the entrances. Once they were seated, the festivities began. Fruit and sweets overflowing silver and golden platters were already in the hall; soon wine and roast meat was served; and, musicians and dancers provided entertainment for their eyes and ears.

The prince noted that the gathered company were drinking down their goblets of wine in one and having never had wine before tried to follow their lead. After a couple of cups of wine, he was alarmed by how the hall seemed to be swaying in his vision and the ever-vigilant Geev noticed his distress and came to his rescue. He told the young prince that the content of his golden chalice was not visible to anyone but the server. He can pretend to drink with the others by bringing the cup to his lips without taking a sip. In this way, only the server, Geev and Gudarz knew how the young prince navigated the challenge of drinking in the company of others without getting drunk. It was growing clear that he needed to master many more skills than those he had thought would define a *pahlevan*.

The morning of the next day, K'Khosro, Gudarz and Geev went sight-seeing around Espahan and took a boat across Zayande-rood. This was such a contrast to the roiling waters of Jayhoon. This was a majestic flow of immense volume, but it exuded peace and prosperity.

The day after, following lunch, K'Khosro was firm in his request to visit with Farigees. Geev knew that he could not put him off this time, and arranged for a meeting room adjacent to the *Serai*. Farigees and

K'Khosro were overjoyed at seeing one another, hugging for a long time and then sat in seclusion to a whispered conversation. K'Khosro had thousands of questions, but was too emotional to remember any. The only thing he did say was: "if becoming the king means being away from you for so long, I want none of it." Farigees assured K'Khosro that she was being well looked after and that he had nothing to worry about. She patiently outlined how protocol and affairs of state would inevitably impact their ability to see one another. She confirmed K'Khosro's suspicions that his rising status would mean more restrictive manacles. He would no longer be free to choose what he does, but obligated to act according to established protocols and the expectations others have of a person in his position. For example, Iranians believe their king is blessed with *farr-e-izadi* – the power to see into the future and to bring about peace and prosperity. Farigees also reminded K'Khosro that his gift is expected to guide his decisions. He should not be seeking consultation with others, as that would be considered a lack of confidence in destiny and fatalism. She warned that any hesitance would severely undermine his capacity to lead. Farigees drove the message home by pointing out that while the Shah of Iran is surrounded by courtiers, he is alone in decision-making and must remain that way.

After reflecting on this conversation, K'Khosro asked: "is that why they have kept us apart since we arrived in Iran?" Farigees explained that this is certainly the main reason they had been kept apart, but that her kinship and religious beliefs were also contributing factors. She went on to explain that being Afrasiab's daughter was a black mark against her. Some people may think that she and K'Khosro are in cahoots with Afrasiab and ascending to the throne would give their enemy another chance to rule over Iran. She also added that her not being a fatalist was also a black mark against her among Iranians. Therefore, if K'Khosro and she kept their distance, her perceived failings would not reflect on him. K'Khosro said that he would do all in his power to dispel suspicions against Farigees and himself. But placing a finger on his lips Farigees replied: "Shush now. You have many more important tasks ahead and once you accomplish them this will take care of itself."

Following their meeting, K'Khosro was unable to focus on anything else for the rest of the day. A day, like so many others, marked by celebrations and countless bombastic speeches by a few who were sober and many more who were inebriated. K'Khosro wondered what are the tasks I am expected to do? What does Farigees mean by saying her allegiance to Iran and K'Khosro would be proven once he was finished? Is she hinting at the expectation that I should avenge my father's death by killing Afrasiab? He had overheard snippets of many conversations about such an expectation among Iranians of all walks of life. This realization was further evidence that he was not free to choose his own path in life and was destined to lead a nation while confined in his actions. He worried again, that an irresistible force was charting his path. Was this evidence of the truth of Zurvan and the Book of Destiny? Or is it a reflection of what people expect of him and how leaders try to meet such expectations? He did not know if it would ever be possible to discern one from the other. He also did not know how to recognize the *farr-e-izadi* that was supposedly the key to being a successful and beloved sovereign.

The festivities in Espahan threatened to go on for an eternity but thankfully ended after seven days with the news that K'Khosro would set off for an audience with Shah K'Kavoos on the next day. K'Khosro initially thought that the travelling party would be Gudarz, Geev, a small contingent of nobility and himself. But in the morning, the air was thick with the sound of horns, drums and hooves of horses getting ready to set off. In all, twelve thousand riders, the nobility and many score in support were assembled outside the city gates. K'Khosro wondered if Gudarz wanted to take the throne by force. When he asked Geev about this, Geev laughed saying: "No. *Farr-e-izadi* has long left K'Kavoos, and he no longer wishes to rule. So, it was not a question of wresting power from a stubborn king but one of a respectful transition." K'Khosro felt that if that was so, why would they be marching there with an army of this size, but he knew that Geev and Gudarz would not be forthcoming with an explanation should he ask.

The trip from Espahan to Abar-kooh, the seat of power chosen by K'Kavoos, took three days. The travellers arrived late at night and camped outside the capital. In the morning, the military contingent stayed behind while K'Khosro and dignitaries entered the city. Their arrival was again celebrated by jubilant crowds who lined the streets leading to the palace. They approached the palace along a broad avenue carved out of stone. The palace itself stood above the city on a rocky outcrop within a walled fortification eight meters tall. Embrasures atop the walls were manned by sentries armed with long-bows. K'Khosro reflected on these embattlements, those around Afrasiab's palace and the simple hut where Chehra and Nozeh lived. He wondered who within each dwelling enjoyed a greater sense of safety and had a sounder sleep?

They entered the palace gate riding their horses but dismounted before climbing the steps to the Royal Reception Hall. They entered according to their rank and stood in line for the king's entrance. Once K'Kavoos entered the room, they all took a knee. K'Kavoos sought out K'Khosro and helped him to his feet. K'Khosro was taller than his grandfather and the king's gate and grip betrayed the frailty that comes with age. He was very emotional at seeing his grandson and thanked the heavens for having been reunited. He then signalled to the others to rise and embraced Gudarz and Geev for their effort to find and return K'Khosro to Iran. K'Kavoos then acknowledged and thanked every other visitor and eventually sat on his throne asking K'Khosro to sit beside him, smiling, crying, and kissing him and murmuring to himself - the only part K'Khosro could discern was "Siavosh". K'Khosro was heartbroken to see a once powerful king now displaying so much fragility. But he also remembered that while he was powerful, he had caused his father to flee his homeland and effectively condemned him to die in exile.

After a while, K'Kavoos regained his composure and asked K'Khosro to tell him about his life and any encounters with Afrasiab. K'Khosro retold his story in great detail, starting with life in Ghalla with Chehra and Nozeh and ending with the crossing of the roiling Jayhoon. He even recalled the encounter with Afrasiab as a thirteen-year-old, pretending to be dim-witted and how Afrasiab was delighted by his nonsensical answers. K'Kavoos listened to his grandson with patience and with his full attention. After K'Khosro had finished, he laid his hand gently on K'Khosro's and said: "All our problems will be put right by you, and you will also avenge the murder of your father."

K'Khosro was proud of his grandfather's interest in his story. But he also noticed that each time he mentioned Farigees, his grandfather could not hide his disdain. This confirmed what Farigees had told him about Iranians' deeply held suspicions about the daughter of Afrasiab. This was a worrying attitude and he wondered how long it would be before people came to meet and know his mother and let go of their suspicions. In the meantime, he wondered how his mother was coping with having to prove herself every day and to keep her distance from K'Khosro to lessen any suspicions directed at him.

This initial get-together between grandfather and grandson lasted a couple of hours and was soon followed by formal celebrations lasting another seven days. Everyone who was anyone in Iran travelled to the capital to attend these celebrations except for three. Zaal who sent his regrets saying he was too frail to travel, Rostam who sent his regrets saying he was busy quelling rebelling tribesmen on the eastern border of Zabolestan and Tous. Tous was the son of Shah Nowzar and the Commander-in-chief of Iran's military forces. He was entrusted with the golden boot and the Royal Standard. He was highly respected by other senior officers and had a distinguished record in fighting and winning many battles. Yet, he opposed the notion of K'Khosro becoming the next Shah. He believed that Siavosh's younger brother Fariborz should succeed K'Kavoos.

After the celebrations, K'Khosro and Gudarz took up residence in Gudarz' estate in the capital. When K'Khosro asked where he might find Farigees? Geev replied in his tone of don't ask and don't seek explanation that, for the time being the lady had decided to stay behind in Espahan.

Chapter 5: Succession

The end of the celebrations also signalled the start of open conflict over who should succeed K'Kavoos. Tous and Gudarz exchanged words that were neither constructive nor appropriate for men of their status. Then they decided that the battle between their two armies should determine succession. So it was that on the next day, the two armies faced off across the vast plain west of Abar-kooh. Pahlevans from each army came forward seeking challengers and the bloody business of war was about to begin when Tous realized that such an action would dramatically weaken the forces of Iran and pave the path to defeat by Afrasiab. So, he halted the madness and suggested that the crown's claimants not fight one another but compete in solving a challenge set by K'Kavoos.

K'Kavoos chose a problem that had befuddled everyone for many years. The inhabitants of the city of Ardebil had been tormented by bloodthirsty *deevs* living in a nearby fort that had appeared over-night. The fort had no gate to ram and walls that had resisted all attempts to climb or penetrate. Occasionally, the *deevs* would descend on the city and abduct some residents to their fort. K'Kavoos declared that his crown should be worn by the one who conquers the fort and frees the good people of Ardebil from their tormentors. Given Tous' insistence that Fariborz had the senior claim to succession, they were given priority in solving the challenge. Should they fail, K'Khosro and his supporters would be given the opportunity to vanquish the *deevs*.

At dawn the next day, horns and drums blaring, Fariborz and Tous' forces rode towards the northwest and Ardebil. The riders were arranged to protect Fariborz with Tous riding at the head of the column in total command. Near Ardebil they found an enormous fort with no openings, not even a window or watchtower. That was strange enough, but they soon found out that they could not even approach the fort for a closer look. The riders that did venture closer soon saw smoke rising from the footfall of their horses and the acrid smell of burning hooves assault their noses. Pressing closer, they found that their armour was growing hot to the point of blistering their flesh. For seven days Fariborz and Tous tried different tactics to reach the fort and failed. Their return signalled to K'Khosro, Gudarz and Geev that it was their turn to try and rid Ardebil from the cursed *deevs*.

Gudarz, wanting to emphasize the status of K'Khosro, ordered they fasten a golden throne atop the largest elephant they could find for K'Khosro to ride on. They arrived outside Ardebil to find an impenetrable fort surrounded by ground too hot to cross. But instead of trying to approach the fort, K'Khosro ordered them to camp at a safe distance. He then asked for a scribe and composed a letter to the *deevs*. In this letter, K'Khosro stated that he was blessed with *farr-e-izadi* and that the Book of Destiny foretold that their fort will be destroyed by his army and they would all be put to the sword; emphasizing that their eradication was Zurvan's will. He then had the letter wrapped around a spear and asked Geev to throw the missile as hard as he could towards the fort. Geev's throw sailed over the high wall.

Not long afterward, an unearthly column of acrid black smoke rose into the sky; the ground surrounding the fort began to cool; and, an open gate appeared in front of their encampment. This sequence of events was more like a dream than reality, but K'Khosro, Gudarz and Geev marched ahead of their army through the gate and into the fort. There, they found a beautiful city. But there was not a soul in sight. This alarmed Gudarz and Geev whose experience in past warfare suggested that this was most likely a trap. They said we know that the *deevs* can make gates appear and disappear at will. They can heat the ground to burn all who approached. Surely, this is a plan to trap and kill us all. They advocated caution and abandoning the fort and camping outside, K'Khosro, atop the elephant and high above the hubbub, was firm in ordering their men to enjoy the bounty they had captured and camp in the city. His demeanor left no room for discussion. Gudarz and Geev knew that opposition was perilous. They believed this to be a trap, their troops believed their success where Fariborz had failed was a sign that the *farr-e-izadi* was with K'Khosro. Questioning K'Khosro at this point would undermine their very attempt to help him succeed K'Kavoos. So, they obeyed and placed their futures in the hands of the young man bestowed with *farr-e-izadi*.

K'Khosro had not been feeling his old self since leaving Abar-kooh. Riding atop an elephant somehow transformed him from a young man who had always obeyed others to one who was issuing orders. He was no longer the boy who would do as bid by Chehra or Farigees. He remembered obeying Nozeh's clipped instructions. He even recognized how he had always followed the suggestions by Geev – delivered in the manner of tutors who could not be denied. But now, he was in command.

K'Khosro had no idea where the notion for writing a letter to the *deevs* had come from. When composing the letter and entering the *deevs'* fort, he had felt the crushing pressure of being responsible for the well-being of his men. But he did not know what had led him to make those decisions. Maybe avoiding conflict was why he came up with the idea of the letter. But strangely, at that time, he was sure he was doing the right thing. And yet, he knew there was no rational reason to be so confident. He wished he could understand the source of this new-found confidence. Was it indeed a sign that he was enjoying divine favour? Would it come and go? If he had it, how could he make sure that he would remain in favour? How could he know what pleased the creator? He was familiar with following the orders of others in the minutest of details. But what were the orders that the creator wanted him to obey? Was the will of the creator some command that would be delivered to him? By whom? Were his thoughts the will of the creator? Would he hear an internal voice? How could he be sure that this is a commandment if the ideas seemed to come from his own mind?

K'Khosro worried that doubt was one way he could fall into disfavour with Zurvan. He vividly recalled that the scribe wrote his letter to the *deevs* on paper made from silk and using ink that had been mixed with powdered gold – as was the custom for *farmans* (decrees) from a king or prince. He had doubted the *deevs* would take a letter displaying such pageantry seriously and wondered if he should be sending them a vitriolic letter instead. He now hoped the creator would forgive his moment of doubt.

Despite that lingering doubt, K'Khosro was certain that by vanquishing the *deevs* of Ardebil he was now one step from being crowned and that he would be even more lonely than ever. His proof was in how Geev and Gudarz treated him after the fall of the fort. K'Khosro would try to ask for their opinions and input into decisions he had to make and their response was only to say "as you wish." The days of conferring and discussing questions seemed to be behind them.

K'Khosro pondering his dilemma by Soheila Haghighat

Chapter 6: A New King for a New Age

The news of K'Khosro's triumph reached the four corners of the land faster than could be imagined. The people of Ardebil thanked him for driving away the *deevs*, but everyone knew that this is the precursor for K'Khosro to ascend to the throne in Abar-kooh. The rest of Iran had not been bedevilled by marauding *deevs* but drought and failing crops had plagued everyone. They hoped that K'Khosro's coronation would bring them rain and prosperity, as well as the security he had won for Ardebil. All along the route from Ardebil to Abar-kooh, the caravan of the prince and his entourage were met with cheering crowds. They saw K'Khosro as a harbinger of a new era of prosperity. The celebrations in Abar-kooh were even more boisterous. Even though only K'Khosro and Gudarz' immediate circle entered the city, leaving their army to camp beyond the city walls, the crowds of well-wishers were so dense that it took hours for the heroes of Ardebil to make their way from the city gate to the palace entrance.

K'Kavoos came as far as the entrance to the Royal Hall where K'Khosro and the party took a knee as soon as they spied his presence. He embraced K'Khosro and bid everyone to stand and enter the Hall. He invited K'Khosro and Gudarz to sit with him on the golden throne. K'Khosro sat to his right and Gudarz to his left. Geev and the remaining dignitaries took their seats around the hall. At that point, K'Kavoos signalled that they would commence the coronation of K'Khosro. He signalled the treasurer to bring the crown and scepter.

Meanwhile, in a voice betraying his excitement and age, K'Kavoos declared that by vanquishing *deevs* K'Khosro had proven that he was blessed with *farr-e-izadi* and the true heir to the kingdom. He had brought peace to the people of Ardebil and now he could do so for the whole nation. K'Kavoos then kissed the crown and K'Khosro's forehead before placing the crown on his grandson's head and declaring him Shah of Iran.

K'Kavoos then declared: "From this moment on, K'Khosro is the Shah of all Iranians. We all pledge allegiance and obey his commands." "However," he added: "let us not forget the hardships suffered by Siavosh and so many others at the hands of Afrasiab..." In his retelling of these tragedies, he constructed a narrative that absolved him of any blame. He continued stating: "Iran and Iranians will not be at peace until the blood of Siavosh has been avenged and the cur Afrasiab has been put to death." Also, pointing to K'Khosro, he added: "This is the first duty of the new shah. So that no one can doubt his true allegiance is to Iran and not to his grandfather in Touran."

K'Khosro rose to thank K'Kavoos for his kind words and exhortations. But as soon as he started to move, he could feel the crown wobbling on his head. He slowed down his movements and kept his head steady while promising to do his utmost to protect Iran and bring prosperity to Iranians. To K'Khosro's surprise the wobbly crown had forced him to act with a new dignity in his movements. He then promised never to forget his enmity with Afrasiab and that he would overcome any obstacle between him and the need to avenge the death of his father.

The festivities began as soon as K'Khosro finished his pledge. At the same time, K'Kavoos quietly slipped out of the Hall. K'Khosro wanted to rush after him and have him stay, but he knew that the crown would fall to the ground if he rushed after his grandfather. Up to this point, K'Khosro had wondered why the crown was so large and heavy. Now he knew, first-hand, that it was designed to dignify the motions of the wearers and dissuade them from sudden and unbecoming behaviour.

With K'Kavoos' departure, the festivities went into high gear. The celebrants displayed an endless appetite for food and drink. They downed the wine in their goblets in one and called for more. Yet, even though it was clear that they were growing more and more inebriated, everyone observed the protocols of court and none had their back turned towards the king at any time. By the same token, no one tried to engage him in conversation. Periodically, they would collectively stop and toast the Shah and he raised his own chalice and joined them. The most pleasant event of the evening, from his perspective, was that the treasurer approached with a bejewelled cap woven from threads of gold and silk for him to wear instead of the unwieldy crown.

As the festivities dragged on, K'Khosro grew tired. He looked about him and saw dozens of large torches illuminating the hall as if it were midday, and remembered how Nozeh would put out the oil lamp in their hut and declare it was time for sleep. He knew he could not put out the torches, so he tried to catch Geev's eye and ask for his guidance. But try as he might, Geev was deep in conversation with friends and family he had

not seen for seven years. So, K'Khosro summoned a
footman to take a message to Geev. Geev came as soon
as asked but wearing a stern look on his face. K'Khosro
was not at all sure that he could get a sensible answer
from Geev when he looked like this. But he was too
tired to care and took the plunge. He asked if it would
be permissible for him to leave the festivities and find a
place to sleep. Geev did not hide his shock at the
suggestion, but remembered the young Shah had never
been exposed to court protocols. He explained that the
host should never turn his back on his guests. Adding
that any festivity would only end when the most
honoured guest stands and asks for permission to leave.
Then there will be one last toast and the host bids
farewell to each guest. Only after all the guests have left
is he free to retire to his quarters.

The most honoured guest on this occasion was Gudarz.
Geev whispered in his father's ear that it was time to go
and K'Khosro performed the expected duties. Then
K'Khosro asked if he could stay with Geev and Gudarz
at their villa to sleep? At which point Geev said: "My
Lord, all of Iran is your home now and you may rest
wherever you wish. But it is normal for you to stay in
your own sleeping quarters in this palace."

Once all the guests had departed, K'Khosro was left with four footmen. They arranged themselves as the four corners of a square with the sovereign in the middle. The front pair led the way towards his private quarters. They crossed several halls and followed endless corridors before reaching their destination. This turned out to be a large doorway guarded by two sentries. They stood aside and opened the doors allowing only the Shah to enter. In his private quarters, K'Khosro found eight more torches, as bright as daylight, in holders too high for him to reach. He was, yet again, denied the calm that comes with darkness and wondered if rulers were ever meant to sleep. But he was too tired and fell asleep on his bed while still wearing the ceremonial clothing of his coronation.

Before dawn, he woke in a cold sweat. He had no idea what was awaiting him on his first day as Shah. No one had told him what was ahead and what was expected of him. All he knew about Iran's rulers were second-hand stories from Farigees who retold what she had heard from Siavosh. He envisioned being draped in a heavy bejewelled gown, sitting on the golden throne with the crown wobbling on his head, receiving an endless train of dignitaries in order of importance from dawn to dusk. They would each be offering him precious gifts and spout fatuous praise and undying fealty. Well, if all he needed to do was to sit and acknowledge these gifts, endure drivel, and smile benevolently, maybe he could act the part.

Before the start of the ceremonies, he thought he should visit with K'Kavoos and apologize for not following him out of the hall the night before. This would also afford him the opportunity to try and get some pointers about his new duties. But when he asked the sentries for the way to K'Kavoos' chambers he was informed that he had not been sleeping there. K'Kavoos had left the palace for his estate in Alborz-kooh before sunset the previous day. Denied the chance to gain pointers from K'Kavoos he hoped to have his mother guide him, so K'Khosro summoned Geev to issue instructions on moving Farigees from Espahan to the palace in Abar-kooh right away. However, he was also thwarted in this. Geev informed him that K'Kavoos' concubines and ladies in waiting had not yet moved from the *Serai* to the Alborz-kooh estate, and Farigees' chambers were not ready for her relocation from Espahan.

The grand reception planned for his first day on the throne was close to the nightmare K'Khosro had envisioned. The first to rise and congratulate the new

Shah and pledging his support was Fariborz. K'Khosro, embraced his uncle and invited him to sit beside him on the throne. He was followed by Tous who, in a tone that barely hid his disdain, offered his congratulations and fealty. Tous offered K'Khosro the Royal Standard and Golden Boot, so that the new Shah could choose his own Commander-in-chief and standard bearer. But K'Khosro returned both to Tous saying he would retain his status as the Commander-in-chief of Iran's troops. After Tous a procession of national dignitaries congratulated the king, offered extravagant gifts and so on. K'Khosro was embarrassed at not knowing most of them. So, he tried to limit his conversations to general platitudes. Much of his focus during this day was also taken up by trying to keep his crown from falling off. It was heavy and unstable. The latter because it was made for a head that was substantially smaller than his. So, he thought, if there comes a day when he can actually give commands, he will have the treasurer alter the crown to fit his head, and he would get housekeeping to install torches on shorter stands so that he could put them out if he should choose to sleep in the dark.

At noon, the stewards ushered the guests to an adjoining hall where tables overflowing with food had already been set. The king was guided to his private dining room, where he ate alone. Not even Fariborz, who had sat by his side all morning, was going to join him at this table. K'Khosro could hear the hubbub of conversations and laughter from next door but his position as shah no longer afforded him the pleasure of being able to break bread with others.

After lunch, just before this reception came to a close, Tous stood up and spoke in a strident tone. He said that K'Kavoos had, in his last decree, ordered us all to prioritize the elimination of Afrasiab over all other matters of state. "You too, your Majesty, promised to pursue Afrasiab and avenge the death of your father and so many more at the hands of this blood thirsty enemy. We stand ready for your command to set off immediately for war with Touran."

This bellicose speech was worse than any nightmare that had disturbed K'Khosro's sleep the night before. If he agreed with Tous, he would be going against his mother's advice of never acting in revenge or anger. If he defied it, he would be breaking his own pledge to K'Kavoos and leave himself open to the allegation that his blood-ties to Afrasiab would prevent him from bringing him to justice. Realizing that K'Khosro had been backed into a corner, Gudarz stepped in saying:

"We all know Tous to be a great warrior and someone who speaks passionately about war. But we need to be patient. Our country has suffered decades of drought and the rains are just beginning. Our men are ploughing the fields to fill stomachs and granaries. We can prepare for war when we are well-fed and can afford to ask our farmers to be warriors. Gudarz continued: "Your Majesty, I implore you to not set off for war in haste. Let us first harvest our fields, rebuild, and make our people prosperous. Only at that time can we attack Touran from a position of unassailable strength." The assembled dignitaries nodded in agreement with Gudarz' measured words and K'Khosro was saved from a perilous situation. Tous and his entourage were visibly upset at this turn of events. But Gudarz had outmaneuvered them and they had to bide their time.

Reception for governors of provinces and mayors of towns from all corners of the land began in the early afternoon. They took up their places in the Great Hall according to their rank and gave endless speeches praising the new Shah. Once their speeches ended a deadly silence fell on the hall and it became clear that the audience were waiting for their sovereign to address them – a message of hope that they could disseminate throughout the realm.

K'Khosro had no experience at making speeches and wished he could disappear, just as K'Kavoos had done. But he stood and, in a voice that was new to him, spoke authoritatively. He thanked everyone for their fealty and support. He then pointed to Gudarz saying that he was the most patriotic and wisest person he had ever met. It is not surprising that when the creator wished to send a message to the people of Iran, Soroush would be sent to Gudarz. The assembled really appreciated this recognition of Gudarz and loudly echoed their sovereign's praise.

Then they all realized that the K'Khosro is still standing and quieted down so that he could continue. K'Khosro continued saying: "... he had never experienced paralyzing fear until he saw a giant of a man approaching him while he was resting beside a stream near Siavosh-Gerd. The giant had a fearsome bushy beard down to his belt and his hand was on the hilt of his sword. I was frozen with fear. Fortunately, as soon as he saw I resemble Siavosh his face softened and I knew I was not in danger. I had heard from my mother that my father had foretold of a *pahlevan* who would come to take us back to Iran. It is difficult to express how grateful I am to Geev for the hardships he endured in the seven years it took to find me in Touran. It is harder still to over-state his bravery in single-handedly fighting and vanquishing those who came to capture us before we could return to Iran. Geev's heroism is why I am standing here. It is not surprising that the wise Gudarz selected Geev as the person to entrust with the heaven-sent task of finding me."

The assembled rose as one in appreciation and celebration of Geev. Again, they noticed that K'Khosro is still standing and they fell into silence in anticipation of the rest of his speech. K'Khosro then said: "The last element in my address is that my priority will be to rebuild our country and address the needs of our people. I shall be travelling throughout the land to lend support in doing so and to hear from the people about their needs and wants. I shall be dedicating all the generous gifts you brought to my coronation and what remains in the treasury to this objective. I am going to entrust Gudarz with overseeing this initiative so that we can attain the prosperity and security that will allow us to battle with Touran and fulfill Tous' vision of avenging our many losses at the hands of Afrasiab." With this, the room erupted in applause.

In the quiet of his bedroom, K'Khosro realized just how much he had learned during that eventful day. Tous' posturing didn't leave much room for reconciliation and friendship. It was clear that Tous would have preferred Fariborz as his sovereign. As Shah Nowzar's son, Tous felt entitled to being prideful and selfish. And as Commander-in-chief of the army, it was no surprise that he favoured war. But being prideful and seeking glory in warfare were a dangerous combination for Tous, his men, and the nation. Gudarz, on the other hand, had proven himself to be measured, calm, politically astute and caring for the people's welfare. He had not hesitated to stand in opposition to a war with such high populist appeal. A course of action which mostly burdened farmers who had to abandon their families and fields to fight wars in far-away places, possibly never to return.

The day had been a lesson in the challenges of being a sovereign and K'Khosro knew that he had much to learn. However, he was pleased that he had, for the second time, accomplished a task that he had never thought he could. He had never spoken in public, let alone to an audience that were older, more experienced, and wiser than himself. But when the audience's eyes were on him, he had found a confident and fluent voice. The expressions he had used were not familiar to him. But their effect on the audience was undeniably positive and greeted enthusiastically. His speech had come from the same inner source that dictated the letter to the *deevs*. Was this inner resource the *farr-e-izadi*?

K'Khosro had no choice but to acknowledge this new force within. He felt it to be a great gift that also entailed significant risks. If he is to listen to this voice in all matters, how can he be sure that he is not making a terrible mistake? For example, what stops Ahriman from impersonating his inner voice and leading him astray? Farigees had told K'Khosro that Siavosh believed that striving to bring prosperity and security to the people was paramount for those blessed with *farr-e-izadi*. But Zurvan warns us that greed is the root of all evil and people should not be encouraged or enabled to seek prosperity beyond their predetermined lot.

As a cautionary tale, Siavosh had spoken of Jamshid. Undoubtedly, a sovereign whose long reign witnessed unprecedented progress across all fields from agriculture to technology and health. His successes also left him believing that maybe he was a deity himself. He ignored Soroush's warnings that overpopulation and over-consumption would doom the country to famine and collapse. As Jamshid's delusions grew, *farr-e-izadi* left him and the country was overrun by Zahhaak's army. Jamshid was slain and the civilization he had laboured to build collapsed.

Yet, K'Khosro struggled with the fact that his own internal voice spoke of working to bring prosperity and peace to his subjects while others insisted that *farr-e-izadi* was with him in order to vanquish Afrasiab and put him to death. K'Khosro could not understand which of these were his true calling? The one that came from within or the one that was expected of him.

This puzzle trapped K'Khosro in another sleepless night and his thoughts spiraled endlessly and never led to anything. In the morning, Geev came to give news that Rostam and Zaal were on their way to Abar-kooh. K'Khosro was ecstatic at this as he had no greater wish than to meet his father's tutors in warfare and philosophy. He hoped they would be able to help him with the puzzle of his inner voice, expectations and *farr-e-izadi*.

Chapter 7: A Fateful Meeting

The next three days of the new sovereign's life were tedious repetitions of the first. K'Khosro really wished for the power to turn back the clock and return to a life of no ceremonies and fewer obligations. The ties that bind rulers were proving to be close to intolerable. Furthermore, he felt that his entourage had trapped him in a golden cage. He was stripped of any freedom to choose and act as he wished. On the morning of the fifth day, came the welcome news that Farigees was now installed in the *Serai* of the palace. As soon as he heard this news K'Khosro rushed to visit with his mother. The four guards at the corners of his throne had no idea what to do. As far as they were concerned, the Shah had receptions to attend. He could not rush to the *Serai* in the middle of the day. So, they stayed glued to their posts. It was against court protocol for the king to leave the Hall of Receptions at this time. There was a standoff. K'Khosro hesitated for a second but then realized that even if he was a slave to the courtiers, his guards had to do as he wished. So, he decided to test the limits of his cage and see if he can begin to wrest back some autonomy. Moving quickly towards the giant doors separating the hall from the private quarters, the guards had no option but to follow and provide protection for their sovereign. Successive sentries along the many hallways were surprised by the approaching monarch and sprang to attention. At the end of the corridor leading to the *Serai* two guards stood to attention and tapped the base of their spears softly on the ground three times, alerting those inside that the sovereign was at their door.

Entering the *Serai* was forbidden to any adult male other than the sovereign. The lady-in-waiting who opened the door had never met K'Khosro and it was her duty to impose the prohibition. So, instead of welcoming K'Khosro, she asked that he step back so that she could confirm his identity with the guards. While K'Khosro could take offence at this, he had come to expect strange rituals at court. What he could not understand was how Farigees reacted to their reunion.

As soon as K'Khosro saw his mother, he ran forward to embrace and kiss his mother, but she stood still and bowed her head instead. He took her hand and asked her about her time in Espahan and journey to Abar-kooh, but only got monosyllabic replies to his barrage of questions. He then spoke of how much he had missed her and her counsel. Then he described his strange trip to Ardebil and the first few days as sovereign. He was hoping she would help him answer the many questions that had come up. But Farigees just gazed into his eyes and stayed silent. K'Khosro finally understood that Farigees was deliberately keeping her distance. He did not know why she would be acting so and wondered if somehow, or something had forbidden her from demonstrating their close bond. So, he realized it was best to keep their meeting short. He took Farigees' hand to kiss before departing. As soon as she realized what he was up to, she withdrew her hand quickly and kept her head bowed until he left the *Serai*.

Seeing Farigees in this condition had a terrible effect on the young sovereign's spirit. He decided to summon Geev and compel him to explain what had happened and why Farigees was so subdued. When Geev arrived, K'Khosro took him to a quiet corner and told him about his visit to the *Serai* and his mother's behaviour during their meeting. Geev, as was his habit, parried the matter saying the she was probably tired from her travels and unfamiliar with her new residence and Ladies-in-waiting.

Unexpectedly, K'Khosro grabbed Geev's arm and asked if Iran was blessed with mountains like Ghalla? Geev thought the young king was thinking about a hunting excursion and said that Iran is blessed with many hunting grounds that are home to games of all kind. He added, there is a splendid spot just north of Espahan. It has high peaks, green pastures and babbling brooks. You can hunt almost anything you desire. K'Khosro asked if there are sheep and goat herding in that region. Geev replied, yes, it is one of the main such centres for the country. K'Khosro waited for a beat and then asked softly: "and how many people stand over these shepherds dictating their every move? Telling them when to raise their hand, or shorten their stride. When they are allowed to smile; how to greet their guests." Geev finally realized what his sovereign was hinting at. He bowed his head and fell silent. K'Khosro continued saying that when recalling his past, only the first ten years of his life in Ghalla have been joyful. I knew my duties for our family but was otherwise free to roam, hunt, and hone my skills. Given what has happened since, the path back to Ghalla is no longer possible. But if I have the option of returning to herding north of Espahan, I would far prefer it to being your sovereign. I do not consent to staying in this gilded cage. I want to take my mother to a place where we can live a simple and happy life.

Geev felt the ground beneath him shake. He had finally understood what K'Khosro was saying and with great effort regained his composure. Quietly he said, being our sovereign is a contract between you and Zurvan. You are blessed with *farr-e-izadi* for as long as you act to improve the lives of those you rule. If you forget that objective your actions will no longer be fruitful and those you love and Iran will suffer. The *farr-e-izadi* parted ways with K'Kavoos because of his insecurity and cruelty. The blessing puts unbounded power at your finger-tips to do good. Acknowledging the source of that power is important. There is no question that few monarchs have done more for Iran than Jamshid. He should have remembered that his success was because of *farr-e-izadi* and refrained from seeking more for his subjects than their allotments. Remember that even the greatest of monarchs have failed when *farr-e-izadi* parts away from them. I believe you have inherited a heavy responsibility from Siavosh and with that the *farr-e-izadi* that he would have been blessed with. Siavosh would never shirk from a challenge that could improve his people's condition. I don't think you will either. I am sorry for not giving you a proper answer for why Farigees behaved as she did. I promise to get to the bottom of this matter and report to you everything I learn.

One day later, Geev sought an audience and reported back about Farigees' life since their arrival in Espahan. He had learned that during Farigees' stay in Espahan, a number of the ladies in Gudarz' *Serai* had quizzed Farigees about her allegiance to Afrasiab and grown confident that she was no defender of that murderous monster. This had pleased them. However, they had been dismayed that she did not believe in Zurvan, the Book of Destiny and fatalism. This had made them all turn against her. Heated exchanges had ensued and the ladies had told Farigees that if the new sovereign is even a little hesitant about *farr-e-izadi* his reign will be ruinous. This was why Farigees has decided to keep her distance. Geev concluded his report by saying: "She is trying to go into seclusion to save you and do what she can to ensure your success."

With each passing day, K'Khosro was growing more restless. Not only was he doubtful about how to recognize the path that *farr-e-izadi* would like him to follow. The constant exposure to the pomp and circumstance of court was giving him the sense that he was no longer in touch with the realities of the world outside. How could he remain confident that he could bring order to the chaos around him and bring about an era of prosperity when he was so out of touch with the world outside . He needed to get away and learn more about his country.

As part of his duties to Iran, K'Khosro knew that he was expected to avenge Siavosh's death. Everyone expected him to capture and kill Afrasiab and his brother Garsivaz. But he also knew that many of the same courtiers who celebrated his coronation and pledged fealty to him had spread false rumours about Siavosh. That the insecure K'Kavoos had turned on him rather than trusted him. So, the people in his court, celebrating his coronation, were responsible for driving Siavosh from his home and birthright. Where should he draw the boundary of blame in avenging the death of his father?

However, every time K'Khosro considered the question of fate, he was reminded of the stuffed toy that Chehra had made for him. His legs would only move when someone pushed them forward. K'Khosro tried to characterize the differences between a monarch in the grip of destiny and that stuffed toy. The only answer he came up with was that the monarch was better dressed. He found it difficult to set aside his free will and accept divine destiny as his fate in all that he would encounter. He did not know how to deny what he was aware of, his own abilities and foibles, and replace it with what he could not understand.

From K'Khosro's perspective, proving his devotion to Iran through bringing about prosperity and defeating Afrasiab were easier than giving himself to fatalism. And Farigees' experience had reminded him that, deep down, the established nobility was very suspicious of him and his mother. Their position was perilous and any misstep could put them in mortal danger. He would need to hide his doubts and prove his love for and selfless devotion to Iran over and over again before he would be considered one of their own and trusted implicitly.

Chapter 8: Zaal & Rostam

After another five interminable days at court, news came that Zaal and Rostam had arrived within a day's travel from Abar-kooh. They had camped there for the night and planned to arrive the next day. After the Shah, Zaal and Rostam were by far the most important and cherished people in Iran. Zaal and Rostam had refrained from visiting Abar-kooh after K'Kavoos had banished Siavosh. This meant that they had not visited the capital for almost twenty years. By visiting now, they were signalling their fealty to K'Khosro and emphasizing that the wait for a sovereign with Divine Blessing was finally over. Every inhabitant of Abar-kooh was excited that their national heroes would be visiting and planned a most spectacular reception in their honour. K'Khosro had his own ideas. He wanted to show his respect for the visitors which meant going to see them instead of receiving them in the capital. The courtiers, weaned on protocol, saw this as a possible affront to the throne and *farr-e-izadi*. Some went as far as suggesting that this would anger the creator and instead of raindrops, rocks would fall from the sky destroying everyone and everything. They argued that Zurvan had willed this world into existence, a misstep by the new sovereign could easily lead this one to be erased and a new one put into its place.

News of deep turmoil at court soon reached Gudarz and Geev who immediately sought an audience with K'Khosro. They asked him to be sensitive to traditions and the importance that courtiers placed in them. He smiled and replied, he is not going to greet Rostam and Zaal as the sovereign but as the son of Siavosh honouring his father's mentors. Gudarz reminded K'Khosro of the deep enmity between Tous and Rostam and that greeting him in this way would be certain to raise Tous' ire. But K'Khosro surprised himself by modifying his argument and saying that Rostam and Zaal were rulers of Zabolestan and his greeting them at their camp is entirely in keeping with court protocols and our equal status. No one could see a way past this deadlock. The courtiers tried to entice K'Khosro to ride on a throne atop an elephant, as he had done to Ardebil, but he asked for Behzad and rode his father's steed to greet the honoured guests at their camp.

The day held two great joys for K'Khosro. First, he was about to meet two of his heroes. Second, by defying court protocols, he had demonstrated that he was not angering Zurvan. This, he hoped, would allow him more latitude to loosen the chains of protocol and have a little more freedom in how he could live.

Farigees had often told K'Khosro that Zaal was probably the most knowledgeable person alive. In the same breath she had also emphasized that Rostam had no equal in military strategy, strength and chivalry. K'Khosro rushed to meet his guests with a heart full of love and a head full of questions. Before the sun was overhead, the two parties met up and before K'Khosro had time to dismount, Rostam and Zaal had both taken a knee. K'Khosro rushed forward, lifting Zaal to his feet and embracing him as his long-lost father figure. He tried to lift Rostam too, but was not strong enough! So, he simply held his arm as he stood. The trio were overwhelmed by their emotions and cried in joy at their long-awaited union. Zaal and Rostam, who could remember the young Siavosh, could not avert their eyes from K'Khosro. He was like a twin of their young protégé. For his part, K'Khosro felt completely at home in the company of his distinguished visitors. His inner voice whispered, as long as these men are with you, nothing can harm Iran.

The party mounted again and rode towards Abar-kooh. The way they were greeted however, was even more heartfelt than K'Khosro's own return from Ardebil. At the royal reception, the visitors shared the throne with K'Khosro and many magnificent feasts and festivities followed.

From K'Khosro's perspective, the ceremonies were to be tolerated, but they were getting in the way of him spending time in private with Zaal and Rostam. In addition, while in the company of others, his guests always kept a respectful distance. He did not know if this was because they were observing protocol, or saw him as a young pretender, or a hangover from their mistreatment by K'Kavoos. Whatever the reason, he was being denied the opportunity to pose his questions to these great men of knowledge and experience, and he longed to be unguarded in their interactions.

Six days after Zaal and Rostam's arrival at Abar-kooh, news came that a band of rebels had taken advantage of Rostam's absence and raided nearby villages. This prompted Rostam to seek permission to leave for home. Zaal also asked if he too should return, but Rostam said that he would be heading directly across mountain passes to put down the rebellion – a two-day short-cut which could be arduous for Zaal. He also reminded his father that once there, he hoped Zaal would not engage in the skirmish as he had not fought for some time. Zaal decided he should travel home at a more leisurely pace when their sovereign gives him leave to return. K'Khosro took advantage of the situation and invited Zaal to stay, saying his father had often mentioned that his year-long stay in Zabolestan had been the most rewarding of his youth and he hoped that if Zaal extended his stay he could also learn from his father's mentor and benefit from his guidance.

Zaal and Rostam were delighted at hearing K'Khosro's heartfelt request. They emphasized that they both lived to serve Iran. After a short pause, Zaal added that K'Khosro as Iran's sovereign had the benefit of the *farr-e-izadi* and as such would not need advice and guidance from anyone else. K'Khosro was hardly able to contain himself. This was the very puzzle that he had been struggling with. Fortunately, he had learned by now that saying so within earshot of others would quickly undermine his reign and the personal safety of Farigees and himself. Instead, K'Khosro apologized and said that he had misspoken. Having only come to learn about *farr-e-izadi* after coming to Iran he was having trouble expressing himself clearly when it came to concepts that his predecessors would have been immersed in since birth. He needed guidance in understanding *farr-e-*

izadi better and hoped Zaal would help with that. On hearing both what was said and had remained unsaid, Zaal replied that he would stay for as long as his sovereign needed him. Then rose abruptly, signalling to K'Khosro that this conversation could only be continued in private.

On the next day, K'Khosro asked Geev, who was now his chief of staff, that he wished to take Zaal to the natural springs near Kalat and Jeram. Geev suggested they delay the trip until it had been properly planned and provisioned. But K'Khosro had grown impatient for meeting with Zaal in private and out of earshot. K'Khosro then proposed that if Geev was worried about their safety, they could travel in a convoy with a dozen outriders ahead and another dozen outriders behind them. Any dangers from front or rear would be met with stiff resistance, and should we be attacked from our flank Zaal and I can keep attackers at bay until you come to our rescue. Geev could see that his sovereign's mind was made up and further objections would be swept aside. So, he set off to arrange for their travel. Observing this, Zaal smiled at seeing the young sovereign growing more confident in taking command.

An hour or so later, the party set off for the Springs. Once the outriders had moved far enough to be out of ear-shot, Zaal apologized to K'Khosro for leaving their meeting abruptly the day before. He explained that one could not depend on the discretion and fealty of everyone, especially at court. In particular when overhearing a conversation, the individual is placed in the position of choosing between their fealty to the sovereign and their belief in the power of the creator. K'Khosro replied, this is exactly the problem he hoped to discuss. I feel that while my coronation was celebrated by all, many still see me as an outsider. The nobility does not know if they can fully trust me. I suspect a deep fissure between those who see us as imposters from Touran and those who believe we belong. The manner in which they reacted to Farigees' beliefs tells me that I am walking at the boundary between acceptance and rejection. If I am seen to waver, even by a single step, from acceptance of divine destiny my support will vanish.

K'Khosro, hesitantly, posed his first question. He asked Zaal if he was right in thinking that religious beliefs were passed on in families and social contexts? Would Farigees' views not be formed by the beliefs that surrounded her in Afrasiab's court and *Serai*? It seems that no one believes in destiny there. Siavosh, on the other hand, was raised in a setting that believes in destiny. Siavosh and Farigees had learned the principles of each belief system from one another, but they had not tried to force their beliefs on one another. However, K'Khosro knew that Siavosh had asked Farigees to teach their son as much as she could about *farr-e-izadi* and the Book of Destiny as these would be critical to his ability to fulfill his role as shah of Iran. Of course, I had heard the two sides of this argument earlier from my foster parents in Ghalla. But in all honesty, I now find myself with the reins of the state without a deep understanding of my subjects' belief system. My subjects believe that I have been gifted with *farr-e-izadi* and the power to do no wrong in bringing them prosperity and security. I feel the test I must pass involves understanding *farr-e-izadi* and how it guides my actions. I don't know what is expected of me and don't trust the source of my inner voice. I know the *farr-e-izadi* can leave the sovereign. I do not want to make any mistakes that could bring that about. If that were to happen, I am even less likely to succeed in fulfilling my responsibilities to the people of Iran.

Zaal began to laugh at hearing this. He then regained his composure and asked for forgiveness. He had no intention of laughing at his sovereign. It was just that K'Khosro had spoken of needing to pass just one test, while Zaal's own life had been a never-ending sequence of tests.

Zaal said: "look at me. I have red eyes, pink skin and white hair. What do you think happened when I was born? The doulas who helped my mother during my birth suspected me of being fathered by Ahriman. News of my birth was kept from my father Saam for fear that he would not only kill me, but also my mother and the messenger. Once Saam had caught sight of me, he was shocked. He was hoping to embrace a beautiful boy. Saam, attributed my birth to an act of vengeance by Ahriman. Knowing that Ahriman had jeopardized all of creation. Saam worried that I would try to destroy his kingdom. However, Zurvan had not killed Ahriman, so he did not kill me. He ordered me taken far away and abandoned in the wilderness. This is how I was taken from Zabolestan to the foothills of Alborz-kooh. The soldiers who left me at the foot of the mountain were hoping I would be taken as prey, or die of cold and starvation. When Simorgh saw me bundled on the ground, she took me to her nest as prey to feed on. But when she tore away my swaddle, she saw an unusual looking child and for an unknown reason decided to raise me instead. I do not owe my life to fatherly love. I owe it to the Simorgh. The rest of my life has been nothing but further tests by people who continue to judge me by my appearance.

Then Zaal asked, do you know the rest of my story? K'Khosro said no and so Zaal continued. Over the years Saam dreamt repeatedly that a horseman brings him news that his son is alive and thriving atop Alborz-kooh. Eventually, he came to the foothills of Alborz and camped there hoping to meet me. The Simorgh was aware of this and thought it was time for me to return to Zabolestan with my father. But I knew no parent other than the Simorgh and had no interest in leaving. The discussion between Simorgh and I was a clash between Simorgh's wisdom and my insecurity. Neither one of us could persuade the other, until Simorgh plucked one of its tail feathers and told me that she would be at my side anytime and anywhere if I ever wished it and set the feather alight. I will do whatever you wish at that time. Even if all you want is to come back and live here. This gave me the assurance I needed to leave the mountain and meet with Saam. My father accepted me and threw his arms around me, but that is also when I was thrown into the crucible of unending tests. Everyone saw me as a strong but wild young man.

No one thought I would be capable of living among civilized people, let alone adapt to a life at court. The courtiers' nickname for me was chicken-bred, I would have dearly liked to see them call the Simorgh chicken to her face. But I proved everybody wrong.

Of course, the one who was most concerned about my return to society was Manuchehr the shah of Iran. He, like all strict followers of Zurvan, was always worried about an attack on his kingdom by Ahriman. He was unwilling to let go of the suspicion that a child who looked like me at birth and raised by the Simorgh was evil by both nature and nurture. He was only convinced of my fealty to Iran when astrologers who had been ordered to look into my future assured him that I was one of the bravest *pahlevans* willing to give my life for the sovereign and Iran.

A few years later, I felt a yearning to go on a hunting trip in Kabolestan. Saam and others warned me off, saying Mehrab the ruler of Kabul was related to Zahhaak the Serpent King. But I was young and reckless and went anyway. I could never have guessed what fate had in store for me. I fell in love with Rudabeh, Mehrab's daughter, and decided to marry her. News of my intention to marry Rudabeh led to a storm of concern at Manuchehr's court. They feared that a child born of the union between the spawn of Ahriman and kin of Zahhaak would annihilate Iran and Iranians. The king, given a history of doubt about me, immediately recalled me to the capital and ordered the high priests to put my belief in Zurvan to the test.

K'Khosro was very keen to learn about the tests that could tell if someone is a true believer in Zurvan. His eyes pleaded for Zaal to continue without leaving out any details.

Zaal continued. As you know, Zurvanism is based on three key principles. First, the principle of time. Everything we experience takes place through time. The creator is outside of time and exercises total control over the orderly sequence of every event through time. Second, the principle of eschewing Aaz and envy and making do with one's allotment. Seeking more than one's lot disrupts the natural balance in the world and leads to its destruction. Finally, the principle of death. Death is the end of our existence in time and there is nothing beyond our allotted time.

The priests quizzed me about these principles for days on end. They posed riddle after riddle all of which were variations on how well I understood and believed the three principles of Zurvanism. For example, they would say: "What has twelve trees each with thirty branches?" Their imagery being an allusion to months in the year and days in a month. Another riddle was: "What happens to a man who comes to a lush field of grass and harvests it for himself?" The answer being that a greedy man may gain temporary wealth but earthly wealth cannot stave off death as prescribed by Zurvan for all creatures.

Zaal shut his eyes to take a break in retelling the story of his inquisition. After collecting his thoughts, he continued: "eventually, the priests attested that I had a deep understanding of Zurvanism." This calmed the waters until K'Kavoos rekindled baseless suspicions about my fealty to the crown and Iran. That is why we broke off relations with the court at Abar-kooh while he remained sovereign.

K'Khosro smiled saying: "Shah Manuchehr and his priests should have known better. I was told that Saam had gathered the best tutors in the land to teach you about the ways of the humans after your return from Alborz-kooh. And, that you had mastered all that they could teach you within three years."

Zaal replied: "That is true. My father did his utmost to help me find my place in human society. But I learned more from Simorgh than any other tutor." K'Khosro interrupted asking: "How did Simorgh know about the ways of humans?" Zaal replied: "The Simorgh perceives the world in ways that are beyond ours. She taught me as much about how to observe the world as I could learn – but I know that my abilities are only a fraction of hers."

K'Khosro asked Zaal to explain what he means by "seeing". Zaal explained that sometimes we choose to see mirages and sometimes a convenient aspect of a problem. Truth lies in seeing all aspects of a problem or spectacle – not one that is shaped by our own interests and expectations. As I am sure you can understand, this is beyond what most people understand as "seeing." K'Khosro admitted that this idea was new to him and asked if Zaal could give an example of what he meant.

Zaal said, people gathered tree branches for fires. They knew how green wood would bend but was hard to break. They also used dried sheep gut for sewing leather and to secure bundles tightly. But it took a person with true vision to put these two observations together and invent the bow, transforming how we hunt for prey and defend ourselves. This example tells us that there are innumerable treasures in our everyday environment, but we are yet to see their true potential and use them to improve our lives.

K'Khosro, mesmerized by the example, asked if this was a skill that one could practice and perfect? Zaal said he knows of no barriers to that, but getting there will take time and patience. Seeing the world is not a skill that can be learned in a day or two or in a class or two. The world, like an onion, had many layers. We need to learn how to see beyond the surface presented to us. Zaal added, beyond patience and practice there is one more condition. That of not holding fast to first impressions. Most people, if not all, form a judgement at the first glance and whatever they see later is interpreted in a way that strengthens that initial judgement. Seeing without taking that first impression as gospel, allows additional observations to help form a truer picture rather than simply confirm that initial, potentially biased, judgement. In holding fast to their first impressions humans are their own worst enemy in learning how to see the world.

The royal party arrived at the springs near midday and Geev greeted K'Khosro and Zaal guiding them to a tent where a sumptuous feast had been laid out for their enjoyment. But K'Khosro was only hungry for learning from Zaal and wondered how, on the return journey, he could ask his questions from this wisest of wise men without appearing to be extremely naïve.

And so, some of the return journey passed in silence. K'Khosro wanted to ask about *farr-e-izadi*, but was fearful that asking any questions could give the impression that he is a nonbeliever. K'Khosro finally thought, maybe the Simorgh's feather is equivalent to having the *farr-e-izadi* and that by asking about the feather he can steer the conversation to fate and enjoying Zurvan's divine blessing.

K'Khosro asked: "Did you ever use the feather to return to Alborz-kooh?" Zaal laughed and said: "I did not use the feather for that purpose, but I did use it to seek help in averting the greatest tragedy I could have faced in my life. Rostam was a very large baby. When Rudabeh was giving birth, she writhed in excruciating pain for more than a day. The doulas tried every trick but the baby was too big to push out. We risked losing both mother and child. In a desperate state, I used the feather to call Simorgh to our side. Moments after setting fire to the feather, Simorgh breezed into the bedchamber. I heard

Simorgh say this child will not be born naturally and must be cut away from his mother. Simorgh instructed us to give wine to Rudabeh so that she would relax and lose consciousness. Then Simorgh directed us on how to cut into her belly so that Rostam could be born and her womb could be sewn up safely. Once Rudabeh woke and saw her baby, she exclaimed: "Well that is a very big boy. I'm so glad he was not carrying his bow and mace with him." After helping with the emergency, Simorgh gave me another feather and said: "your son will be the source of much pride for you and your country...and I will be by your side whenever you need me"

Zaal continued: "There is no question that Simorgh saved us that day. But everything happened so quickly that I don't know if it was a dream or real. I never understood how I thought of seeking help by setting fire to the feather. Was it my own initiative or was it an idea that the Simorgh put into my head? I don't understand how the Simorgh could have travelled so quickly between Alborz-kooh and Zabol. Did her foresight lead her to travel to Zabol ahead of time so that she could be there when needed?"

Destined to Lead?

In hearing "I never understood..." K'Khosro found his opening to ask about his own doubts. He said, I too have had two similar experiences. I don't know how it was that I decided to ride Behzad across the Jayhoon at full flood. In doing so, Behzad swam across with the flow of the river and refused my attempts to change course. In Zam, the nobility declared that the only reason I succeeded in crossing the roiling Jayhoon was because I was blessed with *farr-e-izadi*. I was not familiar with this concept and wanted to reply by saying that the credit should go to Behzad. But thankfully, I never said so out loud. Later, when we were trying to drive out the *deevs* outside Ardebil, I don't know how I thought of writing them a royal decree, implying that I was blessed with *farr-e-izadi*. Again, after Geev's spear delivered the decree to the *deevs*, they fled. Everyone said this is a sign of my divine blessing. I am told that all our futures are already pre-determined and detailed in the Book of Destiny. I am told that the creator bestows *farr-e-izadi* on a worthy individual who is chosen to lead the people. I am supposed to have this gift, but wherever I look, I don't see any sign of a book or a guide to what to do next and how to solve the next challenge.

Zaal raised his hand to signal K'Khosro to calm down and listen. He said, the *farr-e-izadi* is neither a person nor an object. It is not something that you can see or touch. It is not something that is easily described. The best way is to think of it as special abilities that are given to you as part of the contract to look after people's welfare as the sovereign. You are tasked with making people's lives better. To bring about their security, and to ensure fair division of nature's bounty. The public believe that this gift is bestowed upon a person from a distinguished bloodline and exceptional personal integrity. They believe that *farr-e-izadi* gives this individual extra-ordinary power to manage their day-to-day affairs. They trust the sovereign to be fair minded and that his judgements reflect what has been recorded in the Book of Destiny. The public supports the sovereign for as long as they believe he has *farr-e-izadi*.

K'Khosro felt that he now had a better understanding of the *farr-e-izadi* and asked if his actions in Ardebil were a sign? Zaal, corrected K'Khosro by saying what happened had been recorded in the Book of Destiny at the beginning of time. It did not need intermediation by *farr-e-izadi* to take place.

K'Khosro then asked if the events he had recalled reflected passages about his life in the Book of Destiny. Zaal, this time impatiently, replied: "As you know, I am not a sovereign and have not been blessed with divine favour. I would not know how it is manifested. I doubt that the popular idea that our destiny is already recorded in a book has validity. One only writes things down when there is a risk that it would be lost or forgotten. Zurvan is all knowing, all-encompassing and infinite . Why would anything be forgotten or hidden? When people talk about the Book of Destiny it is to conjure a familiar image for an extremely challenging concept. An image that everyone can understand.

K'Khosro still had many questions but they had arrived back at the palace in Abar-kooh. He expressed his gratitude to Zaal, saying this was the most precious day in his life and that he had learned much from their conversation, adding that he felt he had so much more to learn. Zaal replied that it is unlikely that anyone had learned everything there is to learn and he is ready to continue their conversations whenever the sovereign so wishes. Zaal added, perhaps we can take a trip to Tappeh-Sukhteh where Siavosh passed the trial by fire. I am sure we will still be able to catch the scent of burnt wood from that ordeal.

Chapter 9: Beyond First Impressions

After returning to the palace, K'Khosro dearly wished he could continue his conversatins with Zaal. However, his duties loomed large and he found himself once again seated at a table for one, while observing his guests eat, drink and be merry. He needed no further evidence than this to confirm his suspicion that while Shahs maintained an illusion of ruling the realm their actions were strictly controlled by the expectations of the realm. Late that night, when guests were tired of revelry and sought permission to leave, K'Khosro could finally retreat to his private quarter. But his mind was in turmoil. Everything he thought of to calm his mind, would transform into another question needing Zaal to help bring it into focus and help him answer. Finally, K'Khosro decided that he should set aside his fear of asking naïve questions and share his thoughts and concerns openly with Zaal.

In the morning, K'Khosro was up at dawn and immediately asked that they prepare for a visit to Tappeh-Sukhteh. Geev was much happier than the day before, because their destination was not far from town and such an outing was unlikely to expose them to security risks. K'Khosro and Zaal reached the periphery of the two mounds of charcoal and ash after a short ride and dismounted. Zaal reached down and grabbed some ash and coal in his hand and kissed it. He did not try to hide his emotions. His furrowed brow and watery eyes reflected his profound sorrow at the death of Siavosh. After a short while, he gently returned the ash and coals to the ground and whispered, these are the remains of the enormous pyre that Siavosh had ordered for his trial by fire.

K'Khosro had heard Farigees' version of this story and judged the time had come to air his most challenging questions. He asked: "was trial by fire really necessary to prove himself innocent?" Zaal was surprised and asked: "Necessary?" K'Khosro said, I heard about this story from my mother years ago and have been thinking about since then. Siavosh knew that he was blameless and innocent of the rumours that had been spread about him. He knew that being pure of heart, the fire would not harm him. Furthermore, Sudabeh had wavered in her accusation before he stepped into the fire. Why was it necessary to go through with the trial when the allegations brought against Siavosh were known to be lies? Why put together such an enormous mound of firewood, set it alight and cross it when the matter was already settled?

Zaal was visibly upset at having this conversation. He said nothing. K'Khosro continued: "Yesterday you told me that to see clearly, one had to consider all aspects of any issue. I would like you to teach me how to see. I have so much to learn from your personal experiences and the lessons that the Simorgh gave you. Safe passage in the trial by fire does not have just one aspect. I have no idea who came up with the notion that fire does not burn the innocent. I don't know how it can be compatible with fatalism. Would belief in Zurvan not imply that the individual is unaware of their own fate? And if they are uncertain about whether innocence will save them from the flames, how could they subject themselves to such a trial? From another perspective, if fate dictates all our actions, how can one assign blame to the individual for any outcome at all? They did not choose their path. They followed the path drawn for them. So, how can they be judged in regards to the path taken?"

Zaal had his eyes shut while listening but was still reluctant to respond. K'Khosro respected the silence, but eventually broke it saying, I think Siavosh also faced a similar situation on another occasion. When he was summoned to Afrasiab's court, he told my mother that he knew he would not be returning home. Why did he not flee or try to save his life. Why surrender so easily? Did he ask why *farr-e-izadi* would help the innocent escape trial by fire one day and subject them to the bloodlust of a crazed ruler the next?

Zaal saw these questions as a direct critique of fatalism and realized that silence was no longer the best course of action. He said: "One of the keys to being able to see more clearly is not to interrogate history about arriving at just outcomes for humans. The way I see it, you are questioning fatalism expecting it to be judicious and fair. You are asking, how could fatalism lead Siavosh, a person of the highest integrity, to such an ending? Your first impression is that an all-powerful entity with the power to pre-determine all outcomes would also be fair.

The truth is that in Zurvanism, humans do not have an elevated place in creation. They are just one creature among others. The existence of humans is an insignificant side-show in the battle between good and evil. The outcome is no doubt desirable for Zurvan but he has many other perspectives to consider and outcomes for humans do not enjoy a special place among the many other concurrent outcomes for all other creatures. It seems to me that your education about our origin is incomplete. You need to learn how humans came to exist so that you can appreciate their insignificance to Zurvan.

Zaal continued: Let me remind you that Zurvan cleaved off the physical world from his infinite body and twelve thousand years from his perpetual existence to set the stage for the battle between Hormoz and Ahriman. They were each given the power to create whatever good and evil they wanted and to fight for supremacy over the world. Whoever won, could reign over the world for the remainder of time. And, Zurvan wished Hormoz to be the ultimate victor and the ruler of the world.

Hormoz and Ahriman had a number of successes and defeats and Zurvan had pledged not to interfere. But after nine thousand years, Ahriman had taken advantage of Hormoz's innate goodness and his victory was close at hand. This is when Zurvan appeared in the field of battle in the form of a pious personage. The personage lived for thirty years. Ahriman tried to corrupt them for thirty years and failed. In anger, Ahriman beheaded them. A drop of their seed fell to the ground where a rhubarb grew. One stalk grew to take the form of a woman, another stalk took the form of a man. They were called Mashyaneh and Mashy respectively. Their appearance in the world was nothing special. Neither Ahriman nor Hormoz created them. They were an accident, outsiders in the war between good and evil. So, when Hormoz met them, he said that he had created all the good things in the world and appealed to them to live a good life. When Ahriman met them, he made a similar claim and encouraged them to live a life of excess. This is how they came to desire more than what they needed. Fifty years later, after they had experienced everything. Nothing new was left to try, so they grew attracted to one another. Mashyaneh became pregnant and gave birth to twins - a boy and a girl. But because of their unbounded gluttony, they ate their children. Hormoz learned of this and told them that children were not food. They then produced six girls and six boys. These seven couples are the ancestors of all humans.

K'Khosro was shocked. "How can the importance of humans be denied? We are constantly reshaping the world." Zaal replied: "Other creatures are doing the same. But the changes they bring about are less noticeable to our eyes. This is an example of how difficult it is to see from different perspectives. Something else that you are failing to see is that in creating this battlefield and era of struggle between good and evil, Zurvan did not delegate any responsibility to humans. Hormoz and Ahriman are the key combatants and their creatures are their soldiers. Humans are neither their creation nor combatant ..."

K'Khosro interrupted Zaal and asked how could we be sure about this? Zaal laughed and said, you only need to pay closer attention to the details we have already covered. When Hormoz and Ahriman visited Mashy and Mashyaneh neither claimed them as their creation. We humans are not soldiers nor weapons, not even the dross, in the battle between good and evil.

They walked together in silence along the gently rising slope of ash and coals. Each footfall was sending up a puff of ash reminding Zaal of the day he had witnessed Siavosh stepping into the fire and the flames shying away from his approach.

It was approaching mid-day and time for them to head back to Abar-kooh. K'Khosro was struggling with how to ask naïve questions without appearing to be a fool. Finally, he mustered his courage and standing in front of Zaal asked his most pressing question: "How has a religion that treats us as shackled to our destiny with every move pre-determined and judged sinful if wanting beyond our need, found such a staunch following?"

Zaal replied, your answer lies in two observations. First, that we all learn our basic beliefs and behaviours as children through mimicking the adults around us. Some of these traits can change as we age, for example we can learn new languages and customs by visiting and living in foreign lands. Other traits do not change, such as our belief in the power of destiny. Because if we ever did doubt the power of destiny, we would not be able to prove whether that doubt is a manifestation of our destiny or a product of free will. Second, that belief in destiny is incredibly valuable to individuals and society as a whole. When people believe that they have been allotted a specific place in the world and that envy and want beyond it are sinful, they are content with their lot. When a society is free from individual actions dictated by greed and envy, it remains tranquil and free from internal strife. When you look carefully at communities that believe in Zurvan, you will notice that unlike others, there are as many strata as there are individuals. These features of belief in Zurvanism are why it has been so successful in capturing the hearts and minds of our people.

Chapter 10: Zaal's Departure

K'Khosro knew that Zaal's presence was the most precious gift he had been given since his arrival in Abar-kooh. He had so much to learn and absorb about the world before being put to ever more challenging tests. At the same time, K'Khosro was aware that Zaal was being kept from the comforts of his own home. He also noticed the envious glances that accompanied them whenever they held one-on-one conversations. It was as if, despite professed adoration and respect for Zaal, the courtiers were growing anxious about too much influence on the sovereign from Zabolestan.

Zaal sensed the rising tension in court. When he spoke with K'Khosro, he was happy to learn that he too had sensed this and in addition was concerned about keeping Zaal away from home for longer. Wanting to spend as much time as possible with Zaal, K'Khosro signalled that he would accompany Zaal for the first half-day of his journey home. He asked Geev to arrange their escort as he had done for their trips before. He also asked him to organize the formal farewells to take place in the palace. This would free him from having the courtiers in tow while riding with Zaal. Geev reluctantly agreed and arranged for a magnificent feast that same evening, celebrating Zaal until late into the night.

At dawn the next day, the caravan heading to Zabol left the gates of Abar-kooh behind with a small contingent of outriders in advance and rear of Zaal and K'Khosro. Again, when out of the earshot of others. K'Khosro thanked Zaal for coming to the capital and guiding him to better understand the world and his obligations. He added that Siavosh had always spoken of Zaal as his spiritual father and he too aspired to call Zaal his mentor. Zaal knew that the young sovereign must have more questions on his mind to be riding with him. So, he asked: "what is on your mind today?" But K'Khosro remained silent.

Zaal realized that K'Khosro's silence is because he is worried that his questions may be blasphemous. So, he went on to say: "There are two issues that you should keep in mind. First, that being able to think is part of what Zurvan has defined as humanity's allotment. If Zurvan did not wish us to contemplate and ask deep questions, we would not have been granted the capacity to do so. So, contemplating a question is not, in itself, blasphemous. Second, that you need to see any question from many perspectives; one perspective may condemn it as profane while another would cherish it as profound.

For example, let's ask why Zurvan would care about destiny but not about fairness? As humans, we have a tendency to want to give ourselves pride of place. But as we discussed earlier, humans are peripheral to the battle between good and evil. Remember that the combatants are Hormoz and Ahriman. Ahriman was created from Zurvan's doubt about wanting to create a world so that he could be worshiped. Remember also, that Zurvan, realizing that Ahriman was growing in his body, deduced that Hormoz, being older, would be born first. So, without being more specific, Zurvan had promised that his first born would rule the world. Ahriman, upon hearing this, cut through Zurvan's body and emerged with his brother and thus claiming, at least a share in, the promised crown. It is hard to overstate how these events impacted Zurvan's perspective on the process of creation. Clearly, leaving matters to take their own course was not leading to outcomes he had desired. So, he decided to describe everything in absolute detail at the moment of creation. He created an arena for the battle between Hormoz and Ahriman. He set aside twelve thousand years for the ebb and flow of their battle and he pre-determined that Ahriman would be defeated at the end of this period.

Hormoz and Ahriman represented Zurvan' wish for creation of good and evil beings. Neither of them created humans. And unlike the beings that Hormoz and Ahriman created, humans were never involved in the battle between good and evil.

Before the battle began, Zurvan gave Hormoz and Ahriman something they could perhaps use to bring them an advantage in their conflict. He gave Hormoz a green branch, Barsam, known to be a powerful force for creating. For Ahriman, he conjured a force from his own being and Ahriman's element, Aaz, the insatiable sense of greed. Hormoz never learned how to harness the power of Barsam, but Aaz was a powerful weapon in the hands of Ahriman.

The ending to the battle between Hormoz and Ahriman is not clear. By many accounts, after succeeding in consuming most of Hormoz' creatures, Aaz turned its attention to Ahriman's forces. In the end, fearing that Aaz would consume him, Ahriman dug a deep hole in the earth to hide.

K'Khosro asked, do you mean at the end of the battle between good and evil only Aaz and Hormoz remained? But how could Hormoz survive such a confrontation?

Zaal replied: "sadly, the ending to the battle between good and evil is obscure. Aaz is so powerful it can consume any creature, good or evil. We don't know what happens to Aaz after Ahriman goes into hiding. Perhaps after consuming everything, it dies of starvation. But that still leaves Hormoz and Ahriman, with the latter in hiding. I cannot tell you how many times I have tried to solve this puzzle, but each time I consider it, I am on a knife edge between belief and blasphemy. Yet, this is a crucial point. Everything we believe, including the concept of destiny, hinges on a satisfactory answer.

Clearly, Zurvan's attempt to bring about a world to worship him had unanticipated complications. These have shaped the foundations for the religion. Outcomes are predetermined at the dawn of time. It is difficult for us to see this as creatures whose lives begin and end within the continuum of time. Remember, Zurvan is an entity that exists beyond space and time, where past, present and future are concurrent.

K'Khosro thanked Zaal for helping him understand why there is such a strong emphasis on destiny among Iranians and why there is an emphasis on people's lot. Fairness is predefined by the allotment meted out by Zurvan to each being – so whatever their lot, it is by definition a fair outcome.

They rode in silence for the rest of the way to the point where they would part company. Zaal tried to dismount and take a knee before his sovereign, but K'Khosro dismounted with him and held him in his arms, thanking him for sharing his wisdom. Zaal then said: I am very glad that you are so focused on the well-being of your subjects. They are conditioned to accept their lot in life. They will lay down their lives if you should so order. For them, your wishes are divine commandments. They need to be protected and your care for them will help with that." He then lent closer and whispered: "I am glad the tests you put me through were easier than the one I had to pass for Manuchehr's inquisition."

Parting with Zaal was very difficult for K'Khosro. But the caravan was patiently waiting to continue their journey to Zabol. K'Khosro and his entourage headed back to Abar-kooh, but every once in a while, he would look back and see the receding dust from Zaal's caravan. Soon after the dust was no longer visible, a whirlwind blew from the south towards K'Khosro and continued in the direction of Abar-kooh, pointing to where he had to lead in steadfast resolution.

Chapter 11: A Glimmer of Hope

The conversations with Zaal left a deep impression on the young king. He had transitioned from being a shepherd's son in a far-off village to being Shah of Iran in a short span. His knowledge of the beliefs of this nation were rudimentary, but every Iranian was willing to lay down his life at his command.

The inconclusive arguments between Chehra and Nozeh had not shed much light on fatalism and the ways of Iranians. His mother had tried to be dispassionate in retelling the lessons Siavosh had wanted passed on, but somehow these lessons were lifeless and more confusing than enlightening. They were from the perspective of an outsider, retelling the life experiences of a person K'Khosro had never met. K'Khosro felt like an imposter, acting as if he accepted Zurvan and the Book of Destiny. Pretending that he understood what others meant when they declared that he was blessed with *farr-e-izadi*. He knew that he was acting out the role of the sovereign and wondered when he would be found out.

Yet, the conversations with Zaal had shed a little light on his troubling questions. Zaal helped him understand three key facts. First, that being able to think was part of human's allottment. Therefore, it was not blasphemous to think about destiny and explore the nature of belief itself. Second, that he should try and observe any issue from as many perspectives as possible. From our perspective, it was natural to assume that we hold a special place in the world. However, humans were incidental to the struggle between good and evil and not at all important from Zurvan's perspective. So, wondering why the religious edicts do not include more elements directed at humans and what humans care about, such as fairness and equity, should not be a surprise. Third, and most unexpectedly, Zurvan was omnipotent but fallible.

K'Khosro was forming a list of the many inconsistencies in Zurvanism. Zurvan was already all there was. Why the need to be worshiped? Is that not in itself a sign of greed? How can one want more when they are already everything? Maybe being seen to be more than everything is the reward. Why would Zurvan want to have lesser beings be in awe of his powers when he also declares envy and greed beyond one's allotment is sinful? How could Zurvan be all knowing if he doubted the wisdom of creating a world of worshippers? How could Zurvan assume that Hormoz would be the first born? It was clear that Hormoz was bested by Ahriman because Hormoz was bound by only doing good. This meant that being cunning and deceitful was advantageous. How can a battle between good and evil be won by good when the advantage lay with the bad? Didn't Zurvan promise not to interfere with their battle and yet present himself as the pious personage to break Ahriman's spirit? Was Ahriman even more clever than Zurvan had imagined?

Why would the all-knowing Zurvan give the hapless Hormoz the green sapling, *Barsam*, a powerful force for creation? Surely, he knew that Hormoz would not be able to put it to good use. By the same token, how much of *Aaz* was within Zurvan himself before being handed to Ahriman? How much remained? If none, why did Zurvan still need a world of worshippers?

These questions swirled around K'Khosro's mind. He could not discuss them with anyone else, as they would consider them to be blasphemous. But the questions also shed light on what Zaal had said at their parting. He had emphasized the importance of K'Khosro being a sovereign who would have the benefit of his people in mind. Did Zaal mean that he was duty-bound to seek more for his subjects? Does that not constitute greed and going against his people's lot? Would he, a grandson of Afrasiab, not be accused of defying Zurvan and leading Iran to ruin?

What was the take away from the reign of Jamshid? During his long reign, he had transformed the land, bringing about more bountiful agriculture and many inventions including building material, wine, armour and more. He had ended famines and made the people free from common diseases. Through his efforts, his subjects had prospered and lived happier and much longer lives. At some point, he began to wonder if he was a divine figure and this success was due to his own supernatural powers. This turned the people against him. When Zahhaak attacked Iran the populace welcomed the invader, unaware of the reign of terror and misery that he would bring.

These reflections shook K'Khosro to his core. His path was far from clear. Fortunately, he had some time to formulate what he should do. After seventeen years of drought the skies had brought gentle rain and the farms and pastures were no longer parched with thirst. People were looking forward to a bountiful harvest and rebuilding their homes and stables. The harvest would feed them and fill depleted granaries. They would be recovering from a long period of misery and already associated their improving fortunes with a sovereign who benefited from *farr-e-izadi*. K'Khosro saw that perhaps he could work to improve his people's lot but be careful not to let any success go to his head.

K'Khosro did not know if his choices would be the will of the *farr-e-izadi* or that his ideas would be helped along by divine interventions. He considered the answer to this question to be of vital importance to his reign. People believed that *farr-e-izadi* would enable their sovereign to achieve goals that lie beyond the ability of mere mortals. However, he was sure that he could not put much store in such popular beliefs.

Revisiting the puzzle of Jamshid, K'Khosro wondered why Zurvan would abandon a ruler who had brought so much peace and prosperity to his people. Then he made another connection. Shah Hushang had also improved the people's well-being. But there was never a mention of *farr-e-izadi* during his rule. Could it be that the very concept of a divine blessing was introduced with the royal dynasty of his ancestors – the Kianis?

When he came right down to it, K'Khosro, son of Siavosh, raised in the modest home of Chehra and Nozeh longed to regain his free will. He did not want his actions dictated by the *farr-e-izadi*. But he was also realistic enough to know that: crossing the Jayhoon, the letter to the *deevs* and his speech at the coronation were not the product of the young man found by Geev only a few months earlier. His struggle was which was more important in bringing peace and prosperity he so much desired to bring to Iranians; freedom of action or supernatural powers?

Chapter 12: Bloodlust

K'Khosro quietly went about his mission of improving the welfare of people all around the country. He used the reserves in his treasury to help fund irrigation systems, roads and repair of forts and homes. The plentiful rains led to verdant pastures and full granaries. Four years of peace and prosperity made many forget the misery of war and loss.

But somehow, being peaceful and prosperous was not sufficient. Once the populace was no longer worried about their next meal, they began wanting more. Talk of avenging Siavosh's death grew from a quiet murmur into a deafening crescendo in a matter of a few weeks. Many were asking, what is K'Khosro waiting for? Is our sovereign trying to divert our attention from the imperative of putting Afrasiab to death by keeping our bellies filled? Again, the suspicion that maybe K'Khosro was in cahoots with his grandfather began to rise its head.

K'Khosro knew that his subjects were all of the opinion that the *farr-e-izadi* would now compel him to take up arms against Afrasiab. Further delay was no longer possible. He sent messengers to all provinces calling for the governors to gather in Abar-kooh with their troops to begin their campaign to conquer Touran and to bring Afrasiab to justice.

In a few short weeks, a large battalion had assembled with regiments from all corners of the nation and set up camp in the plains outside Abar-kooh. Their generals were housed within the fort. The last contingent was from Zabolestan. They had their own skirmishes to the east and Rostam and Faramarz came to lend moral support before heading off towards India. Once they all gathered, K'Khosro called a meeting of the generals and began to lay out the details of his plan of attack.

K'Khosro began by describing the overall movement of troops. He said that they would be moving along a north-easterly route to the border with Touran, crossing Jayhoon where Afrasiab will no doubt have set up defensive forces commanded by his favourite champion – Belashan. He continued: "Once one of our *pahlevans* defeats Belashan, his forces will scatter to the winds. I have a great prize in mind for whomever challenges Belashan. Who will it be?" The generals whispered to one another in consultation and Bijan, Geev's son, volunteered to challenge Belashan.

K'Khosro continued. Our next challenge will be to defeat Tajaav and his army. They keep watch on the western border of Touran. Afrasiab is very close to Tajaav and attended his posting ceremony in person, and called him the Champion of pahlevans in Touran. Again, K'Khosro asked for a pahlevan to step forward when they faced Tajaav. There were murmurs in the hall and again Bijan volunteered to be K'Khosro's pahlevan in that confrontation.

K'Khosro went on to say, somewhat sheepishly: "Bijan, be careful, Aspanoo, a woman of unparalleled beauty and exceptional skill fights beside Tajaav. Whenever he is in trouble, she comes to his rescue. I have no doubt that she will try to intervene in your fight. Don't kill her. Capture her securely using the gentlest means possible." At this, the generals tittered. What is this all about? Is our sovereign sweet on this woman? How would he know about her? Bijan stepped forward saying he would do as his sovereign pleases.

K'Khosro continued by detailing how, on the route between the border and Touran, their troops will have to go through the pass on Kasseh-river. He then said that Afrasiab had ordered the pass to be piled high with dry logs. His plan was to fall back in front of the invading army, lure them into the pass and then set fire to the pile and burn them alive.

He asked for volunteers to scout the location and set fire to the logs before the army advanced to that position. This time Geev volunteered for this hazardous mission, saying that his familiarity with the country and its language would give him an advantage no one else enjoyed.

Next, the sovereign ordered the caravanserais along the route from Touran to Abar-kooh be stocked with a number of fresh horses, so that messengers could switch to fresh horses at each station, bringing news of the front to the capital as quickly as possible.

Up to this point, the generals were mightily impressed by their sovereign's detailed knowledge of and plan for the campaign to defeat each challenge ahead. They sensed that he had seen the future ahead with great clarity. Yet, their approval turned into near rebellion at hearing his next decrees.

K'Khosro next said: "Now that we have discussed some key aspects of the campaign we need to turn to our obligations to our troops." He then outlined how he wanted each combatant to be a compensated volunteer for the campaign and not press-ganged into service. He said, any soldier in the regiments outside the city wishing to return home should be allowed to do so without any repercussions. By the same token, anyone volunteering to give their lives and livelihood for the campaign ought to be compensated. So, make sure that the families of your soldiers are well cared for and their means remain the same as they would be should their breadwinner not have volunteered.

This last decree crystallized the value K'Khosro placed in establishing and protecting the rights of his subjects. The governors and generals were used to press-ganging farmers into serving them as soldiers. They believed the serfs should be proud to serve their country. So, the generals turned to Tous to express their opposition to this last decree. Tous began to rise in objection but faced such a withering look from K'Khosro that he quickly sat down. With this, everyone acquiesced. After all, only someone with *farr-e-izadi* could know so much about the details of the battles ahead and plan so carefully to assure desired outcomes. No mere mortal could challenge K'Khosro.

At dawn the next day, K'Khosro saluted the generals, cavalry and soldiers heading to war with Afrasiab. At the head of the column, Tous, wearing his golden boot, and Fariborz carrying the royal standard. Their route to the Northeast took them past Kalat. K'Khosro knew that his half-brother, Forood, had fled Afrasiab and established his household near Kalat. K'Khosro worried that Forood would not know about their campaign against Afrasiab and may think that the approaching army is from Touran to capture him. So, he instructed Tous to take the route east from Kalat and avoid approaching Forood's refuge. Sadly, Tous thought he knew better to take his army along a longer route along a dry desert when he could cut their journey short by going past Kalat. This is how tragedy struck long before they faced Afrasiab's forces.

The news of an army entering the Kalat valley caught Forood by surprise. He knew the advancing army would easily overwhelm his meager forces and began worrying about the safety of women and children. He asked his mother, Jarireh, what she thought would be the wisest course of action. Jarireh, was Piran's daughter and Siavosh's first wife. She was wise and measured in her actions. She reassured Forood that his half-brother would never send an army to over-run their fort. She said: "These forces are on their way to battle with Afrasiab and free Touran from that tyrant. I think we should invite their generals to share a meal with us and that you also join their cause. Take Nakhar with you. He knows many of Iran's generals and can vouch for us. That will assure them that we mean them no harm. Go! Ask for Bahram! K'Khosro considers him to be as close as a brother. Invite them to break bread with us."

Forood and Nakhar rode to the peak of Sepeed-kooh. From their vantage point they saw a long column, many rides across, slithering along the valley floor towards them. Their own position on the peak was reported to Tous who ordered Bahram to ride to the peak and capture the lookouts. Bring them back alive for interrogation if you can otherwise, bring back their heads. Bahram rode to the peak and demanded the on-lookers to identify themselves. Forood laughed and replied: "Kalat is our home and we have the right to be here. But let us be more cordial. I am told that there is a pahlevan among you called Bahram who is like a brother to K'Khosro. Our sovereign is my half-brother and we would like to invite the generals of this army to join us in a feast at the fort.

Bahram, upon hearing this, softened his voice, lowered his shield and said: "I am Bahram. I need you to prove to me that you are Forood. If you are indeed related to our sovereign, you should have the Kiani birthmark on your arm." Forood showed Bahram his birthmark and gave him his golden mace as a peace offering to take back to Tous.

Bahram rode back to carry news of their invitation to Tous. But before he could speak, Tous asked, you neither brought them back as prisoners nor are you carrying their heads on stakes. You say that he is a prince – so am I. I suspected that you and your kin are incapable of taking orders. He dismissed Bahram and refused to listen to the message he was carrying. Then called for volunteers among his own troops to go to the peak and bring back the heads of the two on-lookers. A few men stepped forward, but Bahram warned them off. He reminded them that K'Khosro had warned us to take the long way around Kalat. He wanted to avoid this confrontation. Tous is asking you to kill his half-brother. We are on this quest to avenge the death of Siavosh. Are you going to spill the blood of Siavosh's son here? On hearing Bahram's pleading, the volunteers stepped back. But then Rieve, Tous' son-in-law, and Zarasb, Tous' son, stepped forward. Forood could see that Bahram was not returning and that these two riders were approaching with ill intent. So, he shot them both with his longbow before they reached their position.

Seeing this, Tous rushed in, blinded by blood-lust and rage. Nakhar recognized Tous and asked Forood to shoot his horse, not the rider. Tous returned to the valley enraged and commanded Geev to take the peak and slay the men there. Again, Nakhar recognized the great pahlevan and told Forood, this is the man who single-handedly defeated Afrasiab's forces when they tried to bar K'Khosro's return to Iran. So, Forood again took careful aim at his horse and sent Geev back to the valley on foot and uninjured.

Finally, Bijan, with Rehham in tow, went to the peak and engaged in a bloody combat with Forood, injuring him. Forood fled to the fort and died of his wounds in his mother's arms. Nakhar placed Forood's body on the throne in the main hall and all the women in the fort took their own lives by jumping from the parapets to avoid falling into the hands of their enemy. Jarireh then gutted all horses, set fire to their palace and used Forood's dagger to commit suicide next to her beloved son.

The Iranian riders broke through the fortification and faced a most tragic scene. Their cheers of victory were silenced by the horror of the scene they faced. At close hand, Tous finally realized his mistake and ordered their bodies washed in rosewater and buried with the dignity demanded by their position. Then he ordered the forces to march on as quickly as possible hoping to put this tragedy behind.

The news of Forood and Jarireh's death reached K'Khosro on the same day. He was plunged into a deep depression. One that he had never experienced before and didn't know how to overcome. Initially, he wanted to rush to the scene and fight Tous in hand-to-hand combat. But soon realized that as the sovereign he could not do that. Next, he wanted to order Tous brought back to the capital in shackles so that he would be publicly humiliated and stand trial. This too was impractical as Tous was critical to his plans for invading Touran. So, he decided that he should bide his time until after the campaign against Afrasiab before demanding that Tous explain his actions and face their consequences. Waiting for such a day was doubly difficult because by now and through Tous' actions K'Khosro had come to despise him more than he hated Afrasiab.

K'Khosro wondered how it was that the forces that were to avenge the death of his father had killed his half-brother and his father's first wife. Farigees had told him of the exceptional beauty and wisdom of Jarireh; of Piran introducing Jarireh to Siavosh so that he could settle down in Touran and feel at home. Of how this had made Jarireh into a pariah among the nobility of Touran. And of how Forood had the same gentleness and good heart that made Siavosh special.

K'Khosro wanted to sit with his mother and cry in her lap and try to gain some perspective and solace in her company. But there too, he was facing another tragedy. His mother was now a shell of her former self. She was a gaunt figure who spent all day in isolation and silent contemplation. She was highly respected but considered an outsider. K'Khosro wondered if the people who had judged Farigees because of her kinship to Afrasiab, would ever fully embrace him as one of their own?

Chapter 13: News from Touran

Geev sent daily updates on the campaign to keep K'Khosro appraised of their progress. After the forces had crossed Jayhoon, the army had engaged in much pillaging and destruction of property. K'Khosro was fundamentally against this. But he also knew that an army on the march in enemy territory behaved in ways that could only be changed by their generals setting a good example. This was not something he could accomplish from far away where he was unable to share in the dread of fear and euphoria of triumph that were part and parcel of war.

He heard that Belashan had ridden to confront the advancing army, calling out for a pahlevan in hand-to-hand combat in the hope of halting their advance. Bijan had accepted the challenge and after an uncomfortably close and bloody fight managed to kill him. The army had then marched on to the head of the Kasseh pass. Geev had already set fire to the pyre there, but it took three weeks for the fire to die out and the ashes to be cool enough for the army to cross into Kasseh valley and continue its march deep into Touran.

As K'Khosro had predicted, they now faced the mighty Tajaav, Afrasiab's son-in-law and keeper of the Western Fort guarding Touran. Again, Bijan had challenged Tajaav and after a lengthy battle injured him when his mace had caught Tajaav on his back. Tajaav had escaped to the fort looking for a fresh horse to ride to the capital and bring news of the advancing forces to Afrasiab personally. At the gates of the fort, Aspanoo had stood barefooted and without her chainmail asking why she had not been asked to fight at his side, and whether she should stay behind and defend the fort.

Looking to the horizon, Tajaav could see Bijan and his riders approaching. So, despite being injured and on a tired horse, he held out his hand for Aspanoo to jump on his horse and flee. They had tried to escape, but their horse had been too tired to carry them far from the clutches of the pursuing riders. Aspanoo had dismounted to give Tajaav an advantage and Bijan had plucked her from the ground without the need to resort to violence or force. Aspanoo was now held at the Iranian camp awaiting the sovereign's next instructions.

K'Khosro had been sending Geev notes of encouragement and congratulations with each returning messenger, but he was uncertain as to the instructions he should send back with regards to Aspanoo. He had spent a lot of his adolescence in the company of beautiful and wise women in *Serais*. So, he was never going to lose his heart to mere looks. However, Aspanoo was different. He had first heard about her in passing from a border guard near Zam. The guard had spoken of the brave, beautiful and powerful woman who always fought alongside Tajaav. K'Khosro had never met her, but had been intrigued by this description. How could one person embody both unparalleled beauty and be peerless in hand-to-hand combat? How can such contrasting characteristics manifest themselves in the same person? K'Khosro's infatuation with Aspanoo had grown with time. He cherished the idea of being with a woman whose hand could caress gently and also wield a sword without mercy.

Among the many challenges the army would be facing in the campaign to invade Touran, K'Khosro noted the need to overcome the brave and capable Tajaav. In assigning a pahlevan to combat with Tajaav, he had realized that Aspanoo will also get involved. Issuing the decree to ensure her safety was his heart yearning to get close to Aspanoo. But now that she was captured and only a messenger away from being brought to Abar-kooh, he questioned the wisdom of such an act. He asked himself: "What do you think she would like to do?"

It was as if he now needed to reject the greatest gift possible. He could order the object of his desire be brought to the capital. But could a woman who fought selflessly beside Tajaav ever have room in her heart for another man? When he thought about it, he realized that he could not condemn Aspanoo to a life in Abar-kooh and the *Serai*. He may have become infatuated with this amazing woman, but what would she experience in being brought there? Would the courtiers treat her any better than they had Farigees? Could he possibly subject another free spirit to the solitary confinement of an outsider in the gilded cage of an Iranian *Serai?* With this K'Khosro realized that he could never impose his dream of loving Aspanoo at the expense of her freedom. His heart tried to vanquish his head for a day longer, but eventually his head won. With a broken heart K'Khosro wrote to Geev instructing him to free Aspanoo and to give her what she needed to live independently wherever she wished to be.

His day of contemplation had introduced another puzzle about the manifestation of destiny. How could his heart and his mind be in such conflict? How could he be almost paralyzed with longing to hold someone in his arms when he was destined to let her go? Why would he be dragged through this miserable experience if his reign is blessed by the creator? The decision to free Aspanoo had a life-long effect on K'Khosro. Worried that his love may go unrequited or that his will may force someone he loved into a life they did not choose, made him love-shy. He longed for having the companionship of a suitable mate, but no longer believed that such a future could be in his destiny.

K'Khosro was still depressed about deciding to release Aspanoo when news came of a major defeat at the hands of Piran. Tous and many of his generals had, in the wake of a minor victory, feasted and drunk to excess. Piran raided their camp late that night, killing many soldiers and generals where they slept. Gudarz, Geev and Fariborz had been sober. They had dragged Tous and a few others out of the camp and fled to the hills.

K'Khosro felt at least partially responsible for this devastating loss. He disliked and distrusted Tous from their very first meeting. That arrogant man had opposed him as the crown prince and done all he could to undermine his reign. He had agitated for an invasion of Touran on the day of his coronation. He was, probably, a source of speculation that K'Khosro was an outsider with fealty to Afrasiab. His arrogance had led to the tragic deaths of Forood, Jarireh and countless other souls who fell at the fort in Kalat. Why was he still carrying the golden boot? Why had he not replaced this cur long ago? For now, K'Khosro send word that the golden boot and royal standard be taken from Tous and given to Fariborz who would assume command of what remained of their forces. Tous was ordered back to the capital to give an account for his actions and be appropriately reprimanded in public.

Meanwhile, Fariborz sent Bahram on a mission to deliver a message to Piran. The message asked the old fox if night-raids were a righteous tactic for such a distinguished general? Piran received Bahram and sent him back with the message that in rebuffing an invasion, all tactics are honourable. But in order to avoid further bloodshed and remembering the generous spirit of Siavosh, he declared a truce lasting thirty days during which what remained of the Iranian forces were to abandon their position and leave Touran. If any troops remained east of Jayhoon, he would see this as a further act of aggression and punish the intruders mercilessly. The remaining Iranian forces took advantage of this opportunity to gather what they could of their weapons and provisions and retreat to the hills where they had a better chance of defending their position.

Meanwhile, Tous arrived at the capital. K'Khosro could not stand to be in his proximity, but he was also mindful of the advice Farigees had given him about keys to a successful reign. She had said that: he would need to be tough and exacting in his demands so that no one would dare refuse them; he would need to banish doubt, as uncertainty would be interpreted as weakness; he should never allow emotions to cloud his judgements; and in meting out punishment, he should be merciful. These pearls of wisdom were far easier said than enacted. He could not hide his anger and disappointment in Tous and had no idea what he would do next.

When Tous entered the Hall of the People, K'Khosro was hard pressed to recognize the arrogant man who had set off to capture and kill Afrasiab a few months earlier. He shuffled forward, no longer the swagger of a Commander-in-Chief. His clothes hung from his frame, gone were the quilted pleats designed to project a muscular physique. His eyes were dull and his skin sallow. This was not the Tous that K'Khosro hated. It was a broken man. But if everyone thought that K'Khosro should avenge the death of Siavosh at Afrasiab's hand, why could he not avenge the deaths of Forood and Jarireh as well as so many other men and women at Tous' hand? Why did he have to be merciful with Tous and vengeful with Afrasiab?

K'Khosro wanted Tous put to death, but again from somewhere deep inside, he heard a voice that said: it is wrong to slay one of royal blood. Tous was a prince, the son of Nowzar, shah of Iran. So, he showed mercy and ordered his land and title be taken and condemned him to house arrest for the remainder of his life.

Initially, K'Khosro was pleased that despite his rage and hatred of Tous he had shown mercy. The courtiers and governors of provinces far and near praised him for showing restraint. However, those in the military were upset. To them, Tous was a commander without equal and a hero of countless campaigns. He had made mistakes. Blood had needlessly been shed, but that was the nature of war.

Chapter 14: The Ebb and Flow of War

With the defeat at the hands of Piran, their Commander-in-chief recalled in disgrace, and their supplies dwindling, the Iranian campaigners were as demoralized as they could get. The thirty days of truce were passing quickly and they needed reinforcements to continue the campaign. But they were also no longer confident in how their sovereign would judge their action in the battlefield from so far away. Recruiting new troops was doubly difficult when it was clear that the officers no longer enjoyed unwavering support from their sovereign.

The generals knew that the only way to restore morale was to recruit Rostam to advocate their cause. Rostam was both respected by the military and loved and trusted by K'Khosro. So, they sent a messenger to Zabolestan, imploring Rostam to go to Abar-kooh and be their advocate at the court of K'Khosro. The campaign to capture Afrasiab was hanging by a thread and would fail with many more lives lost if they did not have the full support of their sovereign.

Destined to Lead?

Rostam rushed to Abar-kooh and was greeted by K'Khosro at the city gate. At the palace, K'Khosro invited Rostam to sit next to him and asked about his visit. Rostam said both he and Zaal wanted to come and see K'Khosro, but that the visit was urgent and Zaal asked Rostam to pass on his message. He is mindful of all the challenges you are facing and remembers you asking him to advise you whenever appropriate. Zaal wanted me to pass on two messages: "First, that one cannot judge the outcomes of war using the same perspectives of everyday life. In war one kills in order not to be killed. Second, that victory in battle stems from unquestioned trust in command. Generals must of course consider all aspects of what they are seeking and their tactics, but they are not responsible for the outcomes. They do not know what has been written in the Book of Destiny. The generals and their troops only know that they are doing the best they can, given all they are aware of."

Before hearing Zaal's message, K'Khosro thought that Rostam was visiting to let him know that he would be heading to Touran to bring victory to the campaign. He now realized that Zaal was inviting him to appreciate the perspective of his generals if he wished the campaign to succeed.

K'Khosro contemplated what he heard and then, with a bitter smile, said he understands Zaal's message and he will follow his mentor's advice. Rostam was pleased to hear this and emphasized its importance in rebuilding the army and boosting its morale. He continued by saying that Tous is a person who has poor judgement in his reactions. His pride prevents him from being thoughtful when facing the unexpected. He is neither measured in rage nor in celebration. His pride was tested by Forood's invitation. His rage exploded at losing his son-in-law. And his pride was wounded when his horse was shot from under him. His judgement was impaired by rage and pride in Kalat. His judgement was impaired again by wine in Touran. Some mistake these excesses as greatness. In fact, they demand much harsher punishment than K'Khosro had meted out. But the problem is that in judging Tous, the other generals are seeing their own actions are also under scrutiny and that weakens their confidence in your support in how they achieve victory in this campaign.

K'Khosro asked if he needed to pardon Tous in order to restore the morale of his forces? Rostam said nothing. K'Khosro asked if he should be apologizing to Tous and restore his command? Rostam replied that it is Tous who should be apologizing to you and seeking forgiveness. But you should restore his command with the condition that Geev be his second-in-command and that Tous only issues orders after conferring with Geev.

K'Khosro could sense his hatred for Tous resurfacing and taking over his calm exterior. In his mind's eye he visualized the bodies of Forood and Jarireh. He remembered Geev's account of the soldiers beheaded and piled high by Piran on his night-raid. He wanted to reject Rostam's suggestion, but a moment of reflection made him realize the wisdom in Zaal's advice. As sovereign he was condemned to wearing masks that hid his own feelings, presenting instead whatever was expected of him.

The next morning, Rostam, Tous and a handful of senior generals came to the Palace for an audience with K'Khosro. When their sovereign entered the hall, they all took a knee. K'Khosro reached for Rostam and helped him stand, then signalled the others to rise. It was clear that Rostam had met and prepared Tous for this occasion with words of encouragement and praise for his leadership. Tous was wearing a simple tunic and projecting a repentant demeanor. At K'Khosro's signal, Rostam took a seat on the right of the sovereign and the others took up their seats around the room. Tous remained standing and asked permission to approach the throne. He knelt before K'Khosro and asked for forgiveness. K'Khosro accepted his apology and invited him to sit to his left. Without hesitation, K'Khosro reminded his audience that the truce with Piran was nearly at an end and that Iran's forces were stranded far from home with dwindling reserves. There was an urgent need for fresh recruits and supplies as well as an experienced campaigner in command. Therefore, Tous would be returning as Commander-in-chief with Geev as second-in-command. We can be sure that the combined wisdom and experience of these two leaders will assure us of success in our campaign against Afrasiab. At the end of this speech, Rostam asked permission to return to putting down the rebellion in Zabolestan and the meeting came to an end.

With Tous back in command, the process of recruiting new soldiers and gathering supplies for the campaign took on a new urgency and not three days had passed before a large army had gathered just north of Abar-kooh. At dawn the following day, the reinforcements paraded before their sovereign and headed to Touran. During the parade, Tous was standing next to K'Khosro. K'Khosro leaned in and told Tous: "Take your army past Kalat. The shorter route will keep them fresh for battle."

Twenty-five days after the cease-fire, Piran received news that fresh troops were crossing the Jayhoon. Piran was saddened that the Iranians intended to continue their campaign and that further bloodshed would be unavoidable. He sent a messenger to the encampment seeking a meeting with Tous in the hope of making a last-ditch effort for peace.

Piran was met by Tous and Geev with the great respect that he was due. He spoke at length about his love for Siavosh and his efforts to save the lives of Siavosh, Farigees and K'Khosro. Tous and Geev also emphasized that Piran was held in the highest regard by K'Khosro. The last thing they were seeking was further bloodshed or indeed his injury. They had no enmity with him, but they needed to capture and bring Afrasiab to justice. Tous told Piran that he could bring lasting peace between Touran and Iran if he apprehended those responsible for Siavosh's death – namely Afrasiab and his brother Garsivaz – and turn them over to Iran.

Tous continued: "I don't expect you to rebel against Afrasiab so, in recognition of your efforts to protect K'Khosro and Farigees, we offer a life of peace and prosperity in Iran instead of confrontation on the field of battle." Piran was incensed by these suggestions. Through gritted teeth he hissed: "I serve my country and not its sovereign. I would never seek peace and prosperity in a strange land and would never betray the soldiers I have trained and fought alongside. You are asking me to be a traitor. All I am is a soldier trying to prevent further bloodshed."

Geev, who had a history of tangling with Piran and his forces, apologized if the offer had offended Piran. He too emphasized that Piran was considered an adversary of the highest integrity and stature by the Iranian forces. He said that he was sad that they would next be facing one-another in the field of battle and personally escorted Piran to the edge of their encampment.

When Piran returned to his camp, he wrote to Afrasiab with the news that a full-scale war with Iran was no longer avoidable and that they should be sending reinforcements and supplies to drive the invaders out of Touran.

On the next day, a grinding war restarted with some days seeing success for Touran while others ended in favour of Iran. Touran was in the ascendance whenever Humaan, Piran's brother, took the field. He was an exceptional warrior and defeated and killed many Iranian pahlevans who challenged him in hand-to-hand combat. Tous then fought with him for a whole day, but neither were able to gain the upper hand. The prolonged war of attrition had a predictable outcome. Touran was able to replenish their forces from close by and with the aid of allies to the east. The Iranians had to maintain long supply chains from west of Jayhoon and eventually conceded defeat and retreated to the foothills of Hamavan. There, they faced shortage of food and feed – an enemy far more powerful than any weapons Touran could wield.

Daily news of the failing campaign prompted K'Khosro to write and ask for help from Rostam. Within seven days of receiving this request, the lookouts at Hamavan saw the purple standard of Rostam's forces. This news brought new life to the camp and hope replaced the despair that had permeated their spirits.

The renewed vigor in the Iranian camp did not escape Piran's spies and he soon learnt that his forces will be facing Rostam. This was a frightful thought for any enemy and their eventual defeat was almost certain. Piran tried to find a peaceful solution to the war and came to parlay with Rostam. Again, he was respectfully met and offered the same conditions for peace. All the Iranians were looking for was capture of those responsible for killing Siavosh. Again, Piran was neither in a position to accept the offer nor in a position to deliver the culprits. The generals parted again with regret that warfare could not be avoided and the needless death of many would follow.

After Rostam joined the Iranian forces, Touran's forces were defeated in every battle. They even recruited champion warriors from India and China, but these too were killed or left the battlefield injured and humiliated. The emperor of China challenged Rostam to combat sitting on an ivory throne set upon a huge elephant, but Rostam pulled him down with his lasso. The imprisoned emperor paid a considerable ransom to buy back his freedom, leaving his elephant and throne behind.

After repeated humiliations, Piran and Humaan fled the battlefield and the remaining troops laid down their arms and begged for mercy. Rostam ordered them to return to their homes.

Afrasiab, weary of Piran's defeat, thought that his own end could be near and needed to plan his escape to a safe haven. He thought he would try one more time to defeat Rostam. He recalled that many years earlier, Rostam had thrown him from his horse and that his out-riders had swarmed around Rostam preventing him from dealing a blow that would surely have been fatal. So, perhaps the Tourani warriors could try and fight Rostam as a swarm rather than in one-on-one challenges. The new tactic was accepted by Touran's generals and Afrasiab suggested they face the advancing Iranians at the foothills of a mountain he knew very well. He thought in case the invaders were defeated all well and good, and if his own forces were in peril, he could escape through a hidden mountain pass nearby that was familiar to him.

The Iranian forces advanced to the Northeast and faced off against the Touran enemy. In the battle that ensued a large number of riders swarmed Rostam, but each time they tried to get close enough to land a blow, he would kill those nearest to him with the sweeping arc of his mace. As more and more fell around Rostam, those farther away realized that this tactic was not going to succeed and fled the field of battle. Afrasiab, observing the failure of his plan from a distance, wasted no more time and took to the hills. His troops then laid down their arms in surrender. The victors searched high and low for the fleeing monarch, but he was nowhere to be found.

Afrasiab's disappearance plunged Touran into chaos. The rest of the country had no stomach for war and they surrendered to the Iranians. Tous and Geev sent news of their victory to K'Khosro who recalled the troops. His only objective in the campaign had eluded them and there was no need for bloodshed when there was no enmity with the people of Touran.

Eighteen days later, the victorious forces returned to Abar-kooh and were met by their sovereign at the city gate. They were celebrated as heroes and feted in the streets. When Rostam dismounted, K'Khosro rushed forward in a most unbecoming way to embrace him and prevent him from kneeling. He then put his hands on the shoulders of Tous, Fariborz, Gudarz and Geev inviting them to rise, praising them individually for their courage and sacrifice and congratulating them on their victories.

K'Khosro then spoke of his profound sorrow at the loss of Gudarz' sons and grandsons in the battle. At this point he was close to adding that the loss was needless and reveal his true distaste for war. But again, an inner voice reminded him that these men of war only know this kind of life and loss. He should not judge warfare as being regrettable as this would demean them as people and their services.

After the speech by K'Khosro, Tous took centre stage and with unexpected modesty said that no one had done more to pluck victory from the jaws of defeat than Rostam. Rostam then signalled for the war reparations to be brought forward. Forty-five elephants laden with treasures advanced and were directed to the treasury, among them the throne of Ivory formerly belonging to the emperor of China.

After the celebrations for the returning soldiers outside the city walls, the generals were invited to a feast at the palace. K'Khosro had noticed that his guests always arranged themselves according to their rank. Those of higher rank would sit closer to his throne and those of lower rank closer to the exit. He had noticed that this hierarchy automatically led to envy and pride. Anyone closer to the throne was prideful and envied by those who were farther away. He thought maybe his guests drink to excess at feasts to mask these feelings. He decided not to sit on this throne, but to circulate among his guests and give them all the chance to be close to him. This finally helped him break the isolation he had felt at such events. It also helped break the stratification that kept his guests from talking to one another. His guests were more talkative now and they seemed to sip rather than gulp their drinks. He then noticed that Tous is standing in a corner accompanied by two family members, but he is not drinking. This reminded him that following the night-raid, Tous, who was famous for his love of wine, had vowed never to let wine pass his lips again. He could see the misery of self-denial in the old general's face. So, K'Khosro approached Tous and raised Tous' cup to his lip, saying he should not punish himself further. At witnessing this scene, the rest of the officers were overjoyed that the rift between them and their sovereign had been healed and the celebrations lasted late into the night.

Chapter 15: The Embers Reignite

Following the victory in Touran, and Afrasiab's disappearance, the cries for bloodlust gradually died down. The costly campaign to Touran was still fresh in everyone's mind and there was no call for a return visit when news came that Afrasiab has resurfaced and begun to reassert his control. This was not enough to rekindle the previous bloodlust, but a minor incident was enough to reignite the embers of enmity and renewed calls for capture and punishment of Afrasiab.

One day, K'Khosro met with some citizens from Aavaan, a hamlet on the border with Touran. They came to ask their sovereign for help. They explained that their once prosperous community was being overrun by wild boars. These were extraordinarily large animals with tusks rivalling those of elephants. The boars were trampling their crops, destroying irrigation channels and impaling livestock on their rampages. The men in the village had tried to trap and kill them but the boars had proven wily and their skins were too tough to penetrate with ordinary arrows. K'Khosro described the plight of the visitors from Aavaan with his pahlevans asking who would volunteer to help the villagers. As usual, Bijan was the first to step forward. K'Khosro suggested that he go in the company of a dozen riders, but Bijan said he would need no help in this trivial challenge. Eventually, K'Khosro persuaded Bijan to take the older and wiser Gorgin with him – not to help in driving away the boars but to bring back news to the capital should any harm come to Bijan. Gorgin accepted his charge, but was upset at this affront. He envied Bijan for having won the hearts of the people and his sovereign by his acts of bravery in the recent campaign to Touran. He felt that he should have been given a chance to show his prowess. And now, he had been reduced to the role of a messenger about Bijan's whereabouts.

The village representatives, Bijan and Gorgin set off for the border the next day. In less than a week Bijan killed the boars and the hamlet's peace was restored. The countryside near there was exceptionally beautiful and rich in exotic game. So, Bijan decided to spend a few extra days in rest and recreation before heading back to Abar-kooh. This fateful decision nearly killed him and reignited the embers of hatred of Afrasiab in Iran.

Unbeknown to Bijan, that region was also frequented by Manijeh, one of Afrasiab's youngest daughters, and her ladies in waiting. As soon as Bijan and Manijeh saw one another, they fell in love and were inseparable. Not surprisingly, news of their romance reached Afrasiab who was enraged. He ordered the lovers captured and brought to the capital. So that he could make an example of them and to avenge the many pahlevans that Bijan had killed in the wars between Touran and Iran.

The lovers were so oblivious to the world around them that they were easily captured and returned to the capital in shackles. Afrasiab had his daughter brought to him first. He stripped her of all her finery and forced her for wear a wool sack. Then he expelled her from the palace, shouting: "You are no longer of royal blood. I have disowned you. I condemn you to live as a beggar from now on."

Then Afrasiab called for Bijan who was brought in, badly beaten and in chains. He said anytime he had refrained from killing an enemy he had regretted that decision – so he ordered Bijan beheaded right there and then. A number of generals drew their swords to fulfill his wishes, but Garsivaz asked them to step back and suggested a different punishment. The sadistic Garsivaz who took pleasure in killing Iranian pahlevans said he thought that hanging Bijan in the public square for all to see would send a far stronger message than beheading him right then and there. Afrasiab accepted his brother's suggestion and asked him to arrange for the spectacle as soon as possible.

Garsivaz ordered the tallest trees be felled from which to build monumental gallows to hang Bijan high above the square so that his body would be visible beyond the city gates. Meanwhile, Piran returned to the capital and upon hearing about Bijan and Manijeh asked for an audience with Afrasiab. At their meeting, he reminded Afrasiab that he had been hasty in killing Siavosh and that killing beloved pahlevans would likely cause another war and bring Touran to the brink of rack and ruin. Maybe instead of hanging him, he should be put into a deep well from which he cannot ever escape. The well would be covered by a boulder that no human could move, leaving a small opening through which he would receive water and food. This arrangement would ensure that Bijan could never again see the light of day and he would rot away where no one can find him – a far more harrowing end than being hanged or beheaded. Afrasiab and Garsivaz accepted Piran's argument and at night, out of sight of any onlookers, Bijan was put into a deep well near the market-place and covered by a large boulder.

Gorgin brought the shocking news of Bijan's capture to the capital as fast as he could. K'Khosro did not know how to react. He had two problems. First, Gorgin's account of Bijan's capture was proof that he had been an eyewitness and failed to step in, allowing his jealousy of Bijan to lead to the capture of a great pahlevan. This was bitterly disappointing. Second, having let Bijan be captured, Gorgin had headed home instead of following the captors to learn of Bijan's fate. K'Khosro now knew that Bijan had been captured, but did not know if he was alive or dead. If he was dead, there was nothing to be done for Bijan. If alive, he would become a bargaining chip in any conflict with Afrasiab. Finally, K'Khosro realised that solving this problem needed both brains and brawn and wrote to Rostam asking for his help.

Rostam hand-picked seven of his most capable pahlevans and planned their travel in the guise of merchants to the capital of Touran. The visitors pitched their tents near the bazaar and began selling clothes, spices and jewels from Zabolestan. Their cover gave them time to learn the lay of the land. They had hoped to find out if Bijan was still alive and if so where he was being held. All they learned was that the building of the gallows had been halted. Did that mean that Bijan was already dead?

Manijeh heard about the merchants visiting from Zabolestan and came to their tents. She was wearing sack-cloth and in bare feet, yet she did not have the carriage of a beggar. She entered the tent overflowing with goods she could never afford and began a tirade against Iranians. She shouted: "Are K'Khosro, Geev and Gudarz asleep? Do they not know what has happened to Bijan? Why have they not come to rescue him? Rostam was not sure who this was. He began to shoo her out saying: "We are simple merchants from Zabolestan and have no ties with Iran, and no knowledge of Bijan and his capture." As she was being escorted out of the tent, Manijeh said: "Don't judge me from my clothes. I am Manijeh, Afrasiab's daughter. Bijan and I are suffering from his outrage at learning that we have fallen in love. He has disowned me and expelled me from the palace. He has put Bijan in a deep well where he is to live out the rest of his life on bread and water, away from sunshine and deep in his own filth."

She continued by saying that she was begging on the streets to get bread and water and push these down a small opening for Bijan's sustenance. Rostam was intrigued by this account but wanted to make sure that Bijan was still alive and that this was not an elaborate rouse to entrap a potential rescue party. So, he asked Manijeh to wait. He sent one of their team to buy a roast chicken and placed his own signet ring in its belly. He then asked Manijeh to take the food to her beloved in the dead of night and report back his reaction. That night, Manijeh took the bundle of food to the well and listened for the reaction from below. As soon as Bijan had found the signet ring his spirit soared and he cried with joy. Manijeh was puzzled by this reaction, but reported back to Rostam what she had heard the next morning and this assured Rostam that Bijan is alive. He next asked Manijeh to gather some firewood near the well and set it alight the next night, so that they could find the well where their comrade was imprisoned. Manijeh did as she was asked and the rescuers found the well. The seven commandos tried to lift the boulder covering the well opening, but failed. So, it fell to Rostam who somehow summoned the strength to push it aside. The team was then able to pull Bijan out of the well and hide him in their camp, returning the boulder to its original position.

Rostam was saddened by the state of his friend. Bijan was a shadow of his former self. Bent over, dirty, and emaciated from his starvation diet, and he was intolerant of any light having been in total darkness for so long. Nevertheless, the rescuers bathed him, cut his hair and beard and dressed him in new clothes. He at least looked reasonable, but it would take far longer for Bijan to become his old self again.

That same night, they struck camp, sending Bijan, Manijeh and Aashkesh towards the border. Meanwhile, Rostam and his remaining team raided Afrasiab's palace before dawn. Bijan was keen to join them, but they persuaded him that he would be more of a liability in his emaciated condition.

Rostam and his crew quietly entered the palace grounds, striking the sleepy guards with their swords and maces. Afrasiab was awakened by the sound of clashing weapons and prepared to come and punish the intruders until he heard the voice of Rostam who was moving through the palace, announcing who he was and inviting anyone to combat. Afrasiab could hear the footfalls of the remaining palace guards running away from the intruders. He deduced that like his guards, the best option for seeing another day was to take flight.

Only a defenceless palace and distraught women and children remained. Rostam assured them they were in no danger and left the palace disappointed that Afrasiab had escaped capture yet again.

At dawn the next day, a furious Afrasiab came out of hiding and called on his generals to mobilize troops to block Rostam's route back to Iran. He said that only the death of these night-raiders would wash away the previous night's ignominy. By mid- day, a regiment of riders were in pursuit with Afrasiab in command. The seven warriors, inflicted heavy casualties on their pursuers. At witnessing the inevitability of defeat, Afrasiab who was full of bluster heading into battle, displayed even greater talent in slinking away when in danger.

The seven warriors crossed Jayhoon without having to look back and were met with jubilant crowds everywhere on their route back to Abar-kooh. They were the heroes who had rescued Bijan – himself a much-loved hero of the war with Touran. Eventually, they arrived at Abar-kooh where they were met outside the city gate by K'Khosro. By now, everyone knew that he would break protocol, in embracing Rostam and he did not disappoint. But, this time, Gudarz and Geev also broke protocol in embracing Rostam. Not long afterwards, the caravan of Bijan and Manijeh also arrived. The sight of Bijan brought tears of joy to all. And taking care that Manijeh would not be forgotten, K'Khosro held her hands and thanked her for her bravery and for staying true to her love. He then signalled the palace treasurer to bring a magnificent necklace to give to Manijeh.

As usual, jubilant crowds lined both sides of the route along the way from the city gate to the palace. There was much celebration at seeing Rostam in the flesh and of having Bijan back from the clutches of Afrasiab. The celebrations then continued in the palace where K'Khosro took Manijeh to the *Serai* and Farigees, reuniting the long-separated sisters.

K'Khosro could not believe his eyes the next day, when, as was his custom, he would visit his mother before attending to the affairs of state. Overnight, Farigees was standing straighter, colour had returned to her cheeks, and she greeted him smiling and throwing open her arms for an embrace. K'Khosro was finally reunited with his mother for the first time since arrival in Abar-kooh.

Chapter 16: Wars Without End

Rostam's audacious rescue of Bijan and the raid on Afrasiab's palace were much celebrated in Iran. Meanwhile, Afrasiab took them as a personal affront, declaring that only a humiliating defeat of the Iranians would wipe away the shame of their outrageous actions. He immediately ordered the conscription of a large army and sent them to the eastern shore of Jayhoon under Piran's command. He also sent messengers to the Raj of India and the Emperor of China inviting them to join forces in teaching the Iranians a lesson in humility.

Upon learning about these developments, K'Khosro had no option but to gather the provincial governors and generals and map out a comprehensive defence against the gathering enemy forces. He asked Rostam to take his forces to India in a show of force that would dissuade the Raj from joining forces with Afrasiab. He sent Aashkesh to Kharazm to block the emperor of China's path to joining Afrasiab's forces. He sent Gudarz and Geev with the majority of Iran's troops to establish an encampment on the western shore of Jayhoon. All the generals were instructed to try to avoid bloodshed and to bring about a resolution to their standoff peacefully if possible.

Destined to Lead?

Geev contacted Piran as soon as he arrived at the Iranian encampment and for two weeks tried to negotiate a mutually acceptable truce. But their conversations were fruitless. Each commander had the highest respect for their opposite number. But they served countries that were at war and their service defined who they were.

The standoff across the Jayhoon persisted for many days because neither commander wished to draw first blood. As time wore on the proud warriors in each camp grew restless and sought permission to call for challengers in hand-to-hand combat. Humaan, one of Piran's brothers, was a respected and accomplished pahlevan, but he had no patience for sitting and staring at his enemy's encampment across the river. Piran allowed him to seek challengers and for four days he called out to the Iranians for a challenger and none came forward.

On the fourth day, Bijan asked his father Geev for permission to answer the call. He also asked if his father would allow him to wear the Siavosh's chest-plate, a gift Farigees had given to Geev. At first, Geev refused both requests, but Bijan was adamant and took his request to Gudarz. Geev finally gave in and the two champions began an epic battle of strength, will, and skill which eventually led to Humaan's death.

With the death of Piran's brother, all hope of peace was lost and another of his brothers, Nastahan, called for combat with the man who had killed his brother. He too was vanquished and killed by Bijan. Piran, grief stricken at the death of two brothers, challenged Gudarz in hand-to-hand combat. He argued that far too much blood had already been spilt and the generals should fight and the victor would walk proud as the winner of this war and save further bloodshed. Their seconds and other generals opposed such an action but the veterans persisted.

At dawn the next day, the two wizened generals fought valiantly until Piran's horse fell to the ground and could not rise again. Gudarz suggested they resume combat after Piran secured another horse but Piran refused and fled into a nearby field of boulders. Gudarz tried to flush him out, but Piran stabbed him from his hiding place. Despite his injury, Gudarz reflexively turned in his saddle and plunged his spear into Piran's heart.

On seeing Piran collapse to the ground, Gudarz dismounted and held his fallen foe in his arms and cried. Here was the lifeless body of a man of immeasurable integrity. A voice of reason that had prevented further cruelties at the hand of Afrasiab. In being the

Commander-in-chief of Touran, He had been both a mighty foe and a mighty friend to Iran and Iranians. Piran's body was washed in rosewater and wrapped in silk before he was laid to rest in a site worthy of monarchs.

The fall of Piran, dispirited Touran's forces and they disbanded, leaving the battleground and returning to their homes. When the news of his death reached Afrasiab, he took off his crown and laid it on the ground ordering everyone who could fight to join him in command of troops that would invade Iran and vanquish them once and for all. Again, an army was mobilized and ready to cross the Jayhoon, attacking the small Iranian encampment that was left in place after Piran's troops had left the field.

Alarmed at the news, K'Khosro again called on his generals to bring their forces to the aid of Gudarz and Geev on the border with Touran. He then joined the new recruits and in doing so raised the morale of the Iranian camp to a new high. Everyone was confident that with the *farr-e-izadi* fighting alongside them, victory would be theirs.

The rapid resupply of the encampment across the river, along with news that both Rostam and K'Khosro were among the combatants prompted Afrasiab to abandon his plan for a lightning-strike across the river and see if he can gain the upper hand through diplomacy and subterfuge. He wrote to K'Khosro chastising him for planning to overrun the country of his birth. K'Khosro replied that he had no interest in the land or treasure of Touran. He only wished to apprehend and put on trial those responsible for the death of his father.

For three days, the two armies faced off without drawing a sword or shooting an arrow. On the fourth day, Sheedeh, Afrasiab's son, asked permission to challenge K'Khosro. Afrasiab in rejecting this request pointed out that kings should only face other kings. But after that, Afrasiab asked Sheedeh to carry another letter to K'Khosro seeking a peaceful resolution to their conflict. He then added that if K'Khosro rejected that overture, Sheedeh could challenge him to battle.

K'Khosro once again emphasized his objective in facing the Touran forces. He did not seek to shed the blood of anyone from Touran in battle. He was only there to see that those responsible for his father's death were captured and judged for their heinous acts. On hearing this, Sheedeh issued his challenge to K'Khosro and left for his own camp. K'Khosro accepted the challenge despite strenuous objections from his generals. After a harsh battle Sheedeh fell at K'Khosro's hand and the opposing armies unleashed their latent rage against one another. Not surprisingly, with K'Khosro, and later on Rostam as opponents, Afrasiab's forces were defeated yet again. Afrasiab fled once more, this time to Balkh, a fort in central Touran where he tried to rally his generals for further confrontations. They persuaded him that the outcome of more battles with Rostam and K'Khosro would be the same and urged him to lay low instead, somewhere far from the reach of Iranian forces and wait for a better opportunity for avenging his losses.

After the forces from Touran laid down their arms and disbanded K'Khosro travelled to Sogdia to thank the forces from Zabolestan, Kerman and Pars for their service and sent them home. He then commanded his remaining forces to follow Afrasiab's trail to Kang. In the dry plains south of Kang his small contingent were surprised to find a much larger contingent of enemy troops lying in wait.

K'Khosro was sure that they would face defeat. Hiding behind some bushes, he dismounted and got down on his knees, pressing his forehead to the bare ground. He then whispered: "Oh Zurvan, the great creator, if seeking revenge is a sin, I submit to defeat in this battle ground." At that same moment, a strong wind began to blow from the Iranian position towards the Touran forces. Strong gusts of wind picked up the dry topsoil and blinded their enemy downwind and saved them from certain defeat.

Separately, Rostam had heard that Afrasiab was again mobilizing an army to battle with K'Khosro. He doubled back with his troops to come to the aid of K'Khosro and joined him in the plains outside Kang. Imagining that K'Khosro's troops would be exhausted and the newly arrived forces would be road-weary, Afrasiab launched a night-raid on their camp. But Rostam had been informed of this plan and their forces had been lying in wait to surprise their attackers. Many of the raiders lost their lives and the remainder retreated.

Two days later, at dawn, a small contingent of riders left the fort and brough yet another letter from Afrasiab, this time addressed to K'Khosro the Shah-of-Shahs. In this letter, Afrasiab spoke of his regrets. He said that he had killed Siavosh because he had been under the spell of a Deev and that enmity between grandson and grandfather is unbecoming. He said that he would accept exile in Kang and relinquish the rest of Touran to K'Khosro if he would end pursuing him. But his pride would not let him end the letter on a note of conciliation. The letter ended with a threat. "If K'Khosro continue his current path, then destiny had demanded that the blood of father and son both be spilled in Touran."

K'Khosro responded in more detail than before. He asked: "How can you kill my father and then call me Shah-of-shahs? How can you chastise me for seeking to bring a monarch to justice when you beheaded Nowzar? Did you not try to kill me before I was born? Did you not have my pregnant mother dragged behind horses to force a miscarriage? Did you not order me killed and incinerated as soon as I was born? Were all these acts out of patriarchal care and kindness? Was it not you who rejoiced at having a simpleton as your grandson when you interviewed me? Piran saved my mother's life. It was he who assured me of a great upbringing by placing me with my foster parents. How can you claim that you have done me any favours as my grandfather? K'Khosro ended his letter, repeating his earlier statement. "I have no designs on land or treasure from Touran. All I want is to apprehend and bring to justice those who killed my father."

Not long after the letter was delivered to Afrasiab, a number of riders joined the Touran forces outside the fort and the trumpets of war signalled the end of truce. The outcome of this battle was predictable. With Rostam by his side, K'Khosro's forces were always victorious. The Touran army was defeated before noon and Garsivaz was captured by Rostam. The Touran army surrendered and the Iranians began searching for Afrasiab once more. His record of winning battles was poor, but he once again proved to be masterful at escaping the fray.

Afrasiab escaped from the fort at Kang using a secret passage and no one heard from him for some time. It was rumoured that he sought support from the Emperor of China and the Raj of India to mobilize an army and take back Touran, but they refused. They even refused to give him refuge, threatening to send him to Iran should he step onto their territories. Not much longer afterwards, rumours circulated that he had died in flight from capture.

The victory in Touran gave K'Khosro time to visit places he had known as a child. His first trip was to Ghalla in the hope of finding and thanking Chehra and Nozeh. He was bitterly disappointed to learn that his foster parents had left Ghalla and that no one knew of their whereabouts. The small hut that he had grown up in was still there however. He ducked inside and saw and smelt the hearth at which Chehra had prepared so many meals. Being inside the hut reminded him of the love he had received from Nozeh and Chehra. He then noticed what looked like an old rag on a shelf near the door. He pulled it down and realized it was the ragdoll that Chehra had made for him. He held it close and fought back his tears. He had spent the happiest times of his life in this small room with its smoke-stained walls. He knew that as sovereign he could not be seen to cry. But it was already too late. Some of the locals had seen the streaks of tears on his cheeks. He gave to them generously and asked them to keep his secret. Then he rode to the camp so that he could cry to his heart's content in the privacy of his own quarters.

K'Khosro was not able to sleep that night. He held the only toy he had as a child. Sometimes it would be by his side and at times on his chest. He could not bring himself to have it any farther. It was a reminder of how far he had travelled and his adventures since the days in Ghalla. Being there, reminded him of the first time he had taken a life. He remembered the look of disappointment from Nozeh. He wondered what

Nozeh would think of him now, when his decisions and actions had led to the deaths of many thousands of souls.

He then remembered the endless arguments about fate and free will between Chehra and Nozeh. He now understood how it was that their discussions never led anywhere. He recounted his own experience in appealing to Zurvan for approval or disapproval of revenge as a motive to continue the battles with Afrasiab. He could see that it was impossible to prove or deny the irresistible march of events according to the Book of Destiny.

K'Khosro did not know who was right, but he had been ruling a population unwavering in their belief in destiny and following his every command as the personification of the creator's plan. Had he not himself asked Zurvan to judge his motivations? After all, the ground had been torn from Zurvan's own body to become the battleground between good and evil. By pressing his forehead to the ground, he had touched Zurvan. But instead of asking for help, he had accepted the outcome of this battle as a judgement on his motivation. Was this the act of someone accepting an inevitable destiny or one who is persisting with his right to choose?

K'Khosro was beginning to conclude that belief in the irresistible power of destiny is a delusion. How could destiny dictate that they pursue Afrasiab but fail to catch him? Was destiny trying to teach him a lesson in humility by having his forces ambushed? Was the windstorm a coincidence? No lesson on humility was worth the thousands of lives lost in a fruitless pursuit that he had been told was his divine destiny.

After his visit to Ghalla, K'Khosro visited Siavosh-Gerd. He visited the villa Siavosh had built and retrieved the remainder of his father's buried treasure. He distributed the treasure among his troops and spent a long time travelling through Touran and getting to know the country and her people. Wherever he went, he was well received for having spared the country from the continued tyranny of Afrasiab. And perhaps, unconsciously he hoped that in one of these towns a tall and beautiful woman would step forward, introduce herself as Aspanoo and thank him for sparing her life.

Chapter 17: Afrasiab's End

After Afrasiab's escape from Kang, he fell out of sight. people accepted the notion that in escaping to a distant corner of Touran he had met his death. But this was not the case. Afrasiab went west from Kang, but avoided the Iranian troops by choosing a route far to the North. Then he circled north along the shore of the Mazandaran Sea. Finally, following the seashore south, between the coast and the mountain of Barda, he found a haven. It had a spring with fresh water and a cave nearby where he could take shelter. There was not a soul in sight. The nearest villages and farms were more than a day's walk away, and it was far from well-travelled routes. So, Afrasiab decided it was a safe place to hide for a while.

Unbeknownst to him, a hermit by the name of Hoom had also chosen to live near there for exactly the same reasons. Hoom spent his days in contemplation and away from the hubbub of people. One evening, he could hear an unfamiliar sound among the familiar sounds of nature around him. It was the unmistakable and unusual sound of a man whimpering. Hoom went to investigate what could be wrong and whether he could be of assistance. As he drew nearer to its source, he could hear that the whimpering was in the language of Touran. Being a little familiar with that language, Hoom realized what he had been hearing was partly self-congratulatory and partly self-pity. These sounds were coming from a well-hidden cave. So, Hoom quietly approached the mouth of the cave to listen more carefully. Now, he could tell that the man making these noises was not in his right mind. In one sentence he would say that no one in the history of Touran had managed to annex so many lands or amass so much wealth. In the next he was chastising himself for being alone and sleeping on the dirt floor of a cave. In hearing these statements, Hoom was left with the impression that this man is either a delusional vagabond or Afrasiab. He stepped inside to see if he should help and realized that this was Afrasiab speaking in his sleep. He took off his turban and tied him up where he lay. As Afrasiab struggled and woke up, he protested asking why he, a poor innocent man, was being tied up? Hoom replied, I know who you are. You beheaded Nowzar, the shah of Iran, personally. You killed your own innocent brother Eghrireth. You ordered your sadist brother, Garsivaz, to kill Siavosh. And there are countless others who were either beheaded by you or at your command. The time has come to feel the cold blade of a sword on your own neck.

Afrasiab realized that he could no longer pretend to be someone else and instead tried to elicit pity from his captor. He asked: "Have you ever met someone who was truly innocent? Yes, I have made mistakes, but I was under the spell of a beguiling Deev." Hoom ignored the pleadings of his captive and focussed on where he should be delivered. Initially, he thought the governor of Barda would be perfect. Then he realized that Afrasiab was so reviled that he may well be killed on site, long before he could answer for his actions to the shah of Iran. Hoom then realized that the monks at the temple of Azar-Goshasp would be ideal custodians of Afrasiab. They were in control of their rage and had close contacts with the court in Abar-kooh. Handing Afrasiab to them would then free him from having to deal with further obligations and consequences.

The route to the temple from the foothills of Barda was an arduous trek. With each step, Afrasiab would moan and complain that he could go no further. As they approached Sheeth Lake, Hoom thought that he could let Afrasiab refresh a little and loosened his restraints. Of course, Afrasiab being the supreme escape artist, slipped off the turban that Hoom had used to tie up his hands and ran into the lake. Knowing that there was only one way for Afrasiab to escape the lake, Hoom stood guard by the edge of the lake to wait out his captive.

While this was going on, K'Khosro was a guest of his grandfather at his Mazandaran palace. Gudarz and Geev had been visiting the temple at Azar-Goshasp and on their way to reunite with K'Khosro at K'Kavoos' palace. Part way, they came across a tall middle-aged hermit who was scanning the horizon around Lake Sheeth. They were puzzled by this picture and Gudarz asked the hermit what was going on? His answer changed everything. Their entourage were instructed to take up sentry around the lake. Geev then rushed to the palace to Alert K'Khosro and K'Kavoos of the imminent capture of their nemesis.

Gudarz' men then set about preparing a make-shift camp by the shore of the lake to host the royal guests. Gudarz assured Hoom that his troops would catch Afrasiab and invited Hoom to rest, but Hoom insisted on standing and scanning the lake to make sure his captive would not escape again. Gudarz explained that the sentries were among the very best in the land and there was no way for Afrasiab to escape, Hoom who was exhausted sat down and told Gudarz how he had come to capture Afrasiab. Gudarz had spent a lifetime trying to capture Afrasiab, but to his surprise he realized that while this story was interesting, he was even more interested in learning about the storyteller's own life.

That night, they prepared a lavish meal for Gudarz and Hoom, but Hoom would only accept a small portion of bread. Gudarz was hopeful that some wine might loosen Hoom's tongue. But Hoom only drank water. Gudarz was finally forced to ask his question directly. He said: "I can understand why Afrasiab was living in the middle of nowhere, but why were you passing through there?" Hoom replied that he was not travelling through Barda. He had been living there for quite some time. Gudarz who thought he had detected an opening said: "I didn't know of any communities near Barda." Hoom replied cryptically: "There are communities everywhere," After that he fell silent. Later, Hoom also refused the comfortable bed and tent that had been prepared for him. He politely thanked Gudarz, and once assured that the sentries would not allow Afrasiab to escape, folded his turban into a pillow and slept next to a nearby tree.

The afternoon of the next day, K'Khosro and K'Kavoos arrived at the lake. At seeing them, Gudarz took a knee. Hoom, standing behind Gudarz, hesitated before also kneeling. K'Khosro ran forward, and as was his habit, raised Gudarz and gently holding Hoom's arm invited him to stand. K'Khosro exclaimed: "You must be the man who finally captured Afrasiab. Something that none of Iran's many seasoned warriors were able to accomplish." Hoom replied: "That may be so, but I am also the one who could not deliver my captive." K'Khosro wanted to console Hoom and was about to say that Afrasiab was a master at escaping, but when he looked into Hoom's eyes fell silent. He felt that this was a face he had known for years and he should be measured in anything he says.

During this exchange, K'Kavoos dismounted and swaggered into the camp, giving Hoom a dismissive look as he passed. K'Khosro who by protocol had to walk beside his grandfather, squeezed Hoom's arm and gently said: "I look forward to hearing the details of this adventure from you. That is, only if you would like to tell me and this is not an order." Hoom, who had appreciated K'Khosro's kindness bowed his head replying it would be his pleasure.

The next morning, K'Kavoos assumed command of the situation. He said it would be most fitting to punish Afrasiab and his brother together. After Garsivaz's capture, K'Kavoos had demanded that he be brought to him. He wanted to exact revenge in the most painful possible way and others were reluctant to oppose the old monarch's demand. K'Kavoos ordered a bull be slaughtered and skinned. Then the wet hide had been sewn onto Garsivaz's back. As time passed, the drying hide shrank, pulling on the stitches in Garsivaz's skin. Garsivaz lived in escalating agony. Now, he ordered Garsivaz' cage be brought from his palace to the lake. His cries of pain and the clanging of his chains could be heard long before the cage was delivered to the lake's edge.

Afrasiab, hiding among the reeds in the middle of the lake, was alarmed at hearing the agonizing cries of his brother from the shore. He was tired, hungry, cold and demoralized and his brother's cries were too much to bear. He needed to get away where he could no longer hear Garsivaz. So, he tried to sneak out of the lake. But the sentries captured him and brought him to the camp. The man in shackles was wearing rags, bony and crestfallen. He looked nothing like the tyrant who had terrorised so many people for so long. K'Khosro could not help but feel pity for him. K'Kavoos, seeing his grandson's demeanor, was outraged. The two argued about mercy and punishment. Afrasiab was asking for clemency, K'Khosro was recounting his many cruelties so that he could own them. K'Kavoos was growing ever more agitated. K'Khosro wondered if he is yet again suspected of being in cahoots with Afrasiab. Sensing this may be the case, he drew his sword and beheaded Afrasiab. The fallen monarch's head rolled along the ground, while his heart pumped blood spurting onto his white hair and the ground around his body. K'Khosro was shocked by this scene. He felt a dark curtain being drawn between him and the world around him. Moments later, K'Kavoos raised his sword and beheaded Garsivaz. This was a blessing for Garsivaz, saving him from a longer and excruciatingly painful death.

Gudarz, Geev and a few other generals had been witnesses. They came forward to congratulate the monarchs on the end to their long-sought quest for justice. But K'Khosro was in daze, seeing nothing other than the blood-soaked remains of Afrasiab and dripping from his own sword. With great difficulty, he gathered himself and ordered Geev to treat Afrasiab's body as they should for a fallen monarch. His body was washed in rosewater, wrapped in silk and put respectfully in a suitable crypt.

K'Khosro's depression was evident to everyone. It quickly tamped down all merriment at the camp. Instead of celebrating the death of their nemesis, they spent the rest of the day in silent contemplation. The only one who could not abide by this was K'Kavoos who, using the excuse of needing to consult with the monks at Azar-Goshasp, left the camp as soon as he could.

That night was the most difficult of K'Khosro's life. He felt that he had been plunged into complete darkness. He was unable to focus on any positive thoughts. After assuring the prosperity of Iranians, the only goal in his life had been to capture Afrasiab. What would he do now? Afrasiab had risen to glory and fallen so low. K'Khosro was thinking if life is pre-destined in Iran, there is no reason for the creator to have a different plan for Touran. By extension, the shah of Touran would also be following the path that was laid out in the Book of Destiny – whether he did or didn't believe in Zurvan. But if so, Afrasiab was not deciding what to do, his actions were pre-determined. Should such a person be held responsible for their actions? Should he have been merciful? Or was *farr-e-izadi* only with him if he avenged his father's death?

K'Khosro could not find a way out of this conundrum. He remembered Zaal's advice about the need to see other perspectives in all situations. But he could not think of any other perspectives. This was one of the challenges that belief in fate would not help address.

These disturbing thoughts drove away any desire for sleep. K'Khosro decided he may be able to calm his mind by taking a walk around the lake. He was about to step out of this tent, when he realized that as soon as he did so, his guards would scramble to attention and insist on following him, waking everyone else in the camp. It was ironic that even as Shah of Shahs he did not have the power and autonomy to leave his bed and enjoy a walk in quiet contemplation.

Chapter 18: A Different Perspective

K'Khosro greeted dawn as a man desperate to leave behind yet another sleepless night. Shortly after breakfast, Gudarz and Geev brought him the daily briefing on the affairs of state. They reported that news of the death of Afrasiab at K'Khosro's hand was spreading quickly through the land. And to expect great celebrations wherever they go next. K'Khosro cringed at the thought. They then suggested that treating Afrasiab to a respectful funeral ceremony would not be a popular move. K'Khosro disagreed. He said the people of Iran may not appreciate this move at this time, but they will in the future. We will give Afrasiab a reverent funeral because that shows our respect for the people of Touran. K'Khosro added: "With this act I am laying the foundations of lasting peace between our two countries." Gudarz and Geev knew that they would not be able to change their sovereign's mind, so they reluctantly left to carry out his wishes.

K'Khosro was looking forward to the day, because he hoped to have an opportunity to continue his conversation with Hoom. He called for Hoom to join him. When Hoom arrived, he was invited to sit next to the sovereign, but this made Hoom very agitated. So,

K'Khosro asked if Hoom would be more comfortable walking with him around the lake? Hoom said he would be much more comfortable walking with his sovereign and so they set off. Once the guards had taken up positions some distance ahead and behind them and were out of earshot, K'Khosro commented that it was astonishing that Hoom would have happened to be walking in such a remote place, late at night to hear and then apprehend Afrasiab. Hoom replied: "It is not so surprising. I have lived in a cave not far from where I found Afrasiab for many decades. You are right that it is a secluded place which hardly anyone visits. But that very much made it the ideal place for me to live and much easier for me to hear Afrasiab's whimpering." Then Hoom went on to describe the details of how he had used his turban to tie-up Afrasiab and his decision to take him to the monks of Azar-Goshasp in order to keep him from likely immediate slaughter at the hands of local officials.

K'Khosro first thanked Hoom for his good deeds and wise decision-making. But then just like Gudarz, he realized that the story of how Hoom came to be a hermit was likely more interesting than the story of Afrasiab's capture. So, he very politely said: "I think your life story is probably much more interesting. If you are willing to share it with me, I would very much like to hear it. I find it fascinating that such a thoughtful person should have chosen to live in such a remote place and forego the company of other people."

Hoom thought for a while and replied: "I will share my life story, but the short answer is that insatiable curiosity is why I became a hermit." K'Khosro was even more intrigued and he asked Hoom to please do him the favour of a longer answer.

Hoom said that curiosity had derailed his life. Instead of just living life, like his many good friends, his curiosity had forced him to think about the meaning of life and its aim. Then in searching for meaning, he had come to some answers that he knew would be unpalatable for his friends. And he also realized that he could not live among his friends and not tell them about his findings – because that would destroy the honesty at the foundation of any lasting friendship. The only path left open to him was to leave the community behind and live in isolation.

Hoom was yet to finish this last sentence when K'Khosro slapped his forehead in recognition. Hoom was taken aback and asked if he had somehow offended his sovereign. K'Khosro, smiling broadly, said: "No, not at all. Ever since seeing you yesterday, I have had a sense of deep familiarity with you. I now know why. Your gestures and manner of speech reminds me of my foster father Nozeh. He too had a soft voice with which he delivered iron-clad reasoning. He tried to get me to think. I was lucky that he didn't just hint at this or that. He tried hard to sate the curiosity that he awoke in me. He would be open to discussions, even if they could be disturbing for me. You should not worry about it either. I spend a great deal of time in search of answers and doubt is never far from my mind."

Upon hearing this, Hoom smiled and after a short silence said: "I sensed that hesitance in your interaction with Afrasiab yesterday and find it very admirable." K'Khosro knew exactly what Hoom meant and dropped his head saying:" If I could, I would have pardoned him." Hoom said, he too had been chastising himself for apprehending Afrasiab. I keep wondering if I could have taught him how to appreciate the beauty of nature around him, I could have helped him live the rest of his life in peace.

After walking a little further in silence, Hoom began to tell K'Khosro about his life. He was from Mazandaran, a province that spans the southern shore of the

Mazandaran Sea. A region where Hindi and Iranian people had lived side-by-side in peace for centuries. Until K'Kavoos' attack on this region, it was peaceful and ruled by Hindi governors. After their defeat by Rostam, there was a period of unrest, but again, the two communities came to live in harmony, this time governed by Iranians.

Hoom continued: "I come from the city of Aradj. Iranians and Hindis live in separate neighbourhoods, but they live in peace. The Hindis are Brahman and the Iranians follow Zurvan. Superficially, the difference between these two religions has little impact on the way people interact with one another.

As children we had friends in all neighbourhoods and were oblivious to religious differences. But as part of the rite of passage to manhood, community elders taught their youth the genesis and principles of their religion. Our first lesson was about creation. We learned about how Zurvan had come to create the world. It was such a fascinating story that we could not wait to tell our Hindi friends all about it. But when we met, we learned that their world had been created by Varuna and then we began to bicker about which creation story was right and which was wrong and which god was more powerful. In the end, differences in religious dogma were even more powerful than the bond between childhood blood-brothers.

This was a very sad state of affairs and one of our Indian contemporaries, a very smart young man by the name of Sanjay, said he knew how to stitch out friendships back together again. He said he knew the differences between the two creation stories and they were easy to reconcile. Each group had been created by a different and all-powerful god. Through time, the realms of the two gods had expanded as populations grew. Eventually, these two realms had come to touch one another in cities like Aradj. Zurvan and Varuna had no desire to bring their creations into conflict so they worked hard to join them seamlessly. Now we lived in a world where we are the creation of one or the other god and living peacefully as neighbours. We all accepted Sanjay's reasoning and were happy to be friends again. We all agreed that Sanjay would be our leader in Aradj.

Initially, I too was convinced by Sanjay's argument. But when I grew more familiar with the fundamentals of fatalism, the idea that Zurvan and Varuna could co-exist, let alone collaborate, was no longer tenable. If I am a follower of Zurvan, there can only be one supreme being and following the missteps when they first created a world of worshipers, we now live in a world where the minutiae of the lives of every creature is pre-determined by Zurvan and cannot be altered. How could Zurvan accept the notion that Aradj is split between those who worship them and those that may worship a different supreme being?

My curiosity prevented me from living with this conundrum. Initially, I thought that the problem lay in my not knowing enough about fatalism. I cornered the elders of our town and peppered them with endless questions. They patiently answered all of my questions, some of which verged on blasphemy. But their answers only convinced me that the life and spirit of all fatalists is trapped in an invisible but tight cage. A cage that restricts everyone to the space they have been allotted for life. I was dismayed by the idea that humans had emerged from the stalks of rhubarbs and condemned to live out a life fully described in the Book of Destiny.

Hoom, then fell silent. K'Khosro asked, did your exploration end there? Hoom said no. I was disappointed, but still held hope that perhaps Varuna would be more convincing. So, I reached out to the Brahman elders and bombarded them with questions.

Their answers were superficially different, but they too effectively restricted believers to a cage of a different shape. It was not as small as the cage where followers of Zurvan live, but they too were restricted to their caste. The differences are small. One believes in a life where greed is a sin and there is no afterlife. The other believes in many lives, each lived as different creatures until a time that the cumulative experience has quenched all sense of envy and greed. Nirvana is only achieved when you have reached the blissful state of not wanting anything.

So, in death too, these religions are only superficially different. Fatalists are met by Vay the god of wind and judgement who binds their hands and feet. Then Zaman (or Time) arrives and sews their eyelids so that they can see no more and are freed from want. Zaman also breaks their arms and legs to prevent them from moving towards or reaching for something they want after death. In short, the Hindus achieve a state of not wanting by living many lives as many creatures until they are pious. Fatalists live one pious life at the end of which their mutilated bodies are unable to see or react to wanting anything.

After another quiet spell, Hoom explained that I was a shepherd and this gave me plenty of time to think. After examining this puzzle from as many perspectives as I could, I realized that if fate is a list of inevitable events but has no aim or objective, people are indeed slaves to their destiny. But if fate is a delusion of our own making due to religious doctrine, it is the cruelest injustice that humans have imposed on themselves.

Hoom continued by saying: "I know that I cannot prove whether destiny is a fact or a delusion. Even if I were to persuade thousands that it is a delusion, the next person can argue that it was in my destiny to prove it to that many people. The only way I could free myself from this cage was to understand how it is built and therefore how it could be dismantled.

K'Khosro who could see his own doubts and struggles reflected in Hoom's life story interrupted asking: "... and did you learn how to free yourself from the cage?"

Hoom answered: "I first thought that I should take my own life by jumping off a cliff. But then I realized that this could be my fate and I did not want to help Vay & Zaman in their duties by breaking my own legs or blinding myself in the fall."

"My next thought was to move to a remote location where there are no other people. Then I would only have to deal with my own destiny – should there be such a thing. I had heard that west of the Mazandaran and north of a mighty river that feeds it, there is a land rich in its natural beauty but uninhabited due to its remoteness. This is how I came to live in the foothills of Barda. Initially, life alone was uncomfortable and I thought living alone in nature was perilous. But through time, I came to understand myself and the nature around me and I am now no longer alone or feel at risk from my surroundings.

K'Khosro asked: "But what happened to the cage?" Hoom said: "I no longer felt a cage around myself. I confess I do not know if it is there or not. But from my perspective, it seems to have disappeared. I can say that if it exists for others, it is built by their own hands." K'Khosro found this response to be too obtuse. He asked that Hoom speak his mind without fear – speaking in tangents would not do.

Hoom continued. "After I was completely used to being alone, I recognized two changes in myself. First, that I was no longer fearful of anything. Second, that I was no longer thinking about the future. I was delighted by feeling safe and secure. But I have to admit that the idea of no longer thinking about the future made me worry at first. I even wondered if I was losing my mind. When I examined all the events of my life, I realized that I had spent my whole life in the anticipation of what the future would bring. This is how I realized that the worry and planning for 'tomorrows' were dictating my life. So, if my mind was capable of eliminating all thoughts about the future, either I was going mad or I would find a way out of the cage. My curiosity peaked and I wondered if there may be other answers to this puzzle."

Again, Hoom fell silent until he could sense K'Khosro's impatience for him to continue. Hoom said: "after a lot of thought I did solve the puzzle for myself. But I am far from certain that my solution will work for others." By this point K'Khosro was visibly restless for Hoom to reveal the solution to his puzzle.

Hoom said: "I think that the future is only a construct of our mind. It does not exist in reality." At hearing this K'Khosro thought that the earth beneath him had given way. Hoom could see that his sovereign was disconcerted, so he carried on in the hope that further explanation would help him regain his equilibrium.

Hoom continued: "As you know, we divide time into three periods, the past, the present and the future. The past is what we have experienced already – so it existed and we can revisit it through memories. The present is what we are experiencing. But what about the future? It is only imagined in our mind's eye, as dreams, as paths to wants and aspirations. It does not exist outside our minds."

After a period of contemplation, K'Khosro asked: "Do you think there is a link between the delusion of a future and the concept of destiny?"

Hoom replied:" Humans are avarice and envious. Their greed is reflected in the imaginary futures they build for themselves. And as you know, insatiable greed pits them against one another. It is my belief that some thoughtful ancestors realized that a stable society needs to limit envy as much as possible. By inventing the genesis story for Zurvan, they proselytize through a narrative that unfettered greed brings the end to the world. But that was not enough of a deterrent, so they created the added delusion of pre-destined allotments for each person. Destiny is a most powerful restraint on people. But sadly, there is a cost.

K'Khosro said: "Your ideas are difficult to accept, but I do not have any reason to reject them. I treasure the opportunity to hear how a thoughtful person goes about trying to solve this puzzle. I wish I could move your refuge to somewhere closer to Abar-kooh as I would very much benefit from having regular conversations with you. But that would naturally mean that you would no longer be living in a splendid isolation of your choosing. Are you interested in rejoining the living?" Hoom laughed and replied: "But I am not alone. I am surrounded by the living. Nature is full of life and wonder. Thank you for thinking I may be lonely. In the company of nature, I am never alone." K'Khosro asked: "do the animals come to visit you? Hoom smiled and replied no. They go about their own lives and I go about mine. But the fog, the sun and the moon are regular visitors." K'Khosro was intrigued and asked: "Please tell me more. How does the fog come to visit? Is the fog your most welcome guest? You mentioned it before the others." Hoom smiled. He said: "Fog is the gentlest of my visitors. It quietly enters my home and slowly envelopes everything in the cave. It has the most delicate embrace, and once I am in its arms, I can leave my body behind and only use my mind to sense the universe.

After hearing Hoom's description of his life, K'Khosro saw his crown as a trinket in comparison to the hermit's freedom from want. He simply said: "I hope that someday in the future I can have the pleasure of meeting you again."

Chapter 19: Condemned to Doubt

The meeting with Hoom left a lasting impression. K'Khosro thought of Hoom as an ancient tree that had weathered many storms but remained firmly rooted with standing proud. He was envious of Hoom for not accepting a life of doubt. That he had decided to address his doubts head on and live with the consequences. A threshold that K'Khosro had yet to cross.

When K'Khosro compared Hoom and Zaal he could see that they both had come to doubt the notion of a predestined life. And, that their machinations had led to the same conclusion that the concept of predestined lives is a delusion. Hoom had openly rejected pre-destiny and condemned himself to a life of solitude. Zaal had refrained from speaking his mind and kept his conclusions to himself. The difference between these wise men was that Hoom rejected a life of insincerity among his friends. He could not bear the idea of wearing a mask of conformity with people whose belief system he thought to be delusional.

K'Khosro was also in awe of how Hoom presented himself as he was. He did not put on airs. He did not offer false praise. He valued truth above all else and the price he paid was solitude. K'Khosro wanted to emulate Hoom. He wanted to pull the curtain aside and show Zurvanism to be a delusion, but he knew that he could not calculate the cost of doing so, let alone pay it.

He knew that at twenty-three he was a young monarch and that turning his back on the world would be possible but challenging. Yet his decision on what to do was made in recognition of Zaal's words. He reminded himself that he cared deeply for his people and that they had submitted themselves to his decision-making as the representative of their destiny. They needed a wise and benevolent ruler to ensure they received their lot in peace and prosperity. So, while doubt continued to cast a deep shadow across his connections to the world, Zaal's comment was a beacon of purpose lighting his path forward.

In recognizing his predicament. K'Khosro realized that he had a duty to his subjects that he could not shirk. So, he devoted himself to rebuilding and revitalizing Iran. He earmarked one-third of taxes from each province (that would usually flow to the capital) to be spent on local development projects. He demanded twice yearly progress reports from each provincial governor to ensure the funds were being put to good use. And so it was that what was started as a three-year initiative became a long-term program lasting many decades during which the people in all corners of Iran grew more prosperous than they had ever been.

In raising the people's standard of living, K'Khosro was giving his subjects more than they could have expected to be their lot. He wondered if this lived experience would undermine the religious tenet that wanting more is a sin. The people believed that K'Khosro's efforts were the source of their new found prosperity. They believed that he had succeeded because of *farr-e-izadi*. They discounted their own efforts and saw their incremental prosperity as Zurvan made adjustments to their lot. To K'Khosro's disappointment nothing was able to shake their tenacious belief in fate.

In the forty-third year of K'Khosro's reign, Farigees was taken ill and she passed away peacefully. K'Khosro saw this as his last real connection to the world and again began contemplating the idea of emulating Hoom. He longed to abdicate his rule and live an honest life in solitude.

By this time, K'Khosro knew that what he intended was far more than his rebellion against protocol. *Farr-e-*

izadi would choose to support a monarch. It would choose to part ways with a wayward ruler. But no ruler had ever turned the tables and chosen to part ways with *farr-e-izadi*.

The idea that he may be able to free himself from his cage gave K'Khosro a new hope and he devised a plan of action. His daily routine for decades had been to sit on his throne, and hear his subjects' news, requests and more in the People's Hall. His first move was to let it be known that he would take a break of one week from holding a public audience. This took the court by surprise. Three weeks later, K'Khosro again declared that he would take a week off. This led to significant agitation and open inquiry as to what was going on in the sovereign's private life to necessitate these week-long absences. The concern grew so acute that Geev went to Zabolestan to alert Rostam and Zaal about the turmoil at court. They returned with Geev to Abar-kooh.

When K'Khosro was informed of Zaal and Rostam's arrival he greeted them as before but his visitors were guarded and tense. Even before they could sit together, Zaal began to address his sovereign: "I have fought for the Shah and Iran my whole life. I have tried to prevent the needless death of Iranians. I tried and failed to dissuade K'Kavoos from attacking Mazandaran. That is where the *farr-e-izadi* parted ways with him. Rostam was still a very young pahlevan, but I did not hesitate to send him to K'Kavoos' aid and he brought him back safe. K'Kavoos' arrogance tempted him to take to the skies. Again, I tried to dissuade him, but failed and he was captured and humiliated. Again, Rostam went to his aid and rescued him. What is wrong with you? Did you inherit the selfish traits of your grandfather? Should we have deduced that your true nature was that of your ancestors? Were you showing your true self when you insisted on fighting Pashang Sheedeh the son of Afrasiab against the advice of your generals? Let me remind you that no monarch enjoying the *farr-e-izadi* has abdicated. Being our sovereign is your destiny and you are forbidden from making such a selfish decision. Stop this foolishness and recognize that you are being misled by a Deev. You are a much-loved sovereign and that is where you are destined to stay and serve.

K'Khosro patiently listened to Zaal's speech and was silent for a short while. Then he said: "I was not expecting such a sharp rebuke from my wise mentor. I am sad that my actions have upset you and Rostam. I am eternally in debt to you both. But let us not forget that I am the great grandson of Fereydoun and Tur, and the son of Siavosh and there can be no shame in my lineage. My mother was Afrasiab's daughter, but she was disowned and endured unspeakable hardship for loving Siavosh and carrying his child. So, there can be no shame in that either. And it was my blade that beheaded that monster. I did so because he was an enemy of Iran. It is true that I accepted the challenge from Pashang against the advice of our generals. But Rostam was not there and Pashang would have killed any other challenger from our camp. So, I am not sure if your criticisms are well grounded."

K'Khosro went on to add: "... for years now, I have had no real purpose and I go through the motions of being the monarch. I am constantly worried that unknowingly and unintentionally I may take a misstep that would lead to misery for my subjects. For years, I have wished that I could be freed from this state of doubt and perpetual anxiety. Five weeks ago, my wish was granted. Soroush came to me in my dream and gave me the great news that the time for my departure has come. I was also informed about what was to come afterwards. Relying on what I have learned I can assure you that the country faces no danger from my abdication. Just as my arrival was cause for great jubilation. I hope that my departure will also be celebrated. Now, you should all come and help with the preparations for that final celebration. We have one more week to enjoy each other's company."

These heartfelt sentiments expressed by K'Khosro disarmed the gathered nobility. And the mention of Soroush was enough to persuade them that their sovereign is the dictates of Zurvan. Who could object to that? Zaal stood up and apologized for his sharp tone, blaming his old age. The others gathered around K'Khosro and said that they would respect his wishes.

After a week of celebrations, K'Khosro ushered the nobility into the People's Hall. He greeted them, inviting Zaal to sit on his right, Rostam on his left, and the others to take up their seats. Then he began by praising the great Gudarz and his service and designated him as his executor. He then issued royal decrees that reaffirmed Zaal and Rostam as rulers of Zabolestan; he reappointed Gudarz and Geev as rulers of Espahan, Tous as Commander-in-chief and Fariborz as the keeper of the Royal Standard.

Then surprised everyone by Lohrasb as his successor. A hush fell over the hall. Zaal, broke the silence saying that many would wonder if Lohrasb has the ancestral pedigree to be our sovereign. Furthermore, he has not proven himself in a way that suggests he deserves to lead us. The others joined in and questioned Lohrasb's selection as K'Khosro's successor. But K'Khosro reminded them that Lohrasb is the great grandson of Hushang and that the Pishdadian were a successful dynasty and presided over Iran's prosperity. In addition, you seem to have forgotten that Lohrasb served bravely, successfully and without fanfare in many skirmishes and in attending to the matters of state in his province. Finally, I think that his son Goshtasb also has the same admirable qualities and I am confident that the rules of Lohrasb and Goshtasb will bring further peace and prosperity to Iran and Iranians.

Zaal, when reminded of the bloodline of Lohrasb, withdrew his objection. He realized that K'Khosro had finally acted on his doubts. The crown would be returning to the dynasty preceeding the Kiani clan. Other dignitaries nodded their approval, but some expressed surprise at K'Khosro's strong endorsement of Goshtasb, who was still a youngster and as yet untested. They asked what it is that K'Khosro sees in this boy. But he did not answer them and did not explain whether this was his wish or a premonition informed by Soroush. They had no idea how much their country would change under the reign of Lohrasb and Goshtasb. That during their reign a prophet by the name of Zoroaster would proselytize a religion that would prove a strong alternative to fatalism. At the end of this tumultuous meeting, Zaal, Rostam and others pledged fealty to Lohrasb and he promised to follow faithfully in K'Khosro's path.

At dawn the next day, a large party of dignitaries gathered at the city gate to bid K'Khosro farewell and ride with him for half a day. He turned in his horse and warned them to return home. He could see that a blizzard was heading towards them. Most of the noblemen turned back. However, Tous, Fariborz, Geev, Bijan and Gostaham continued to follow K'Khosro as he rode in a north-easterly direction towards the highest peak in Iran – Sepeed-kooh. K'Khosro turned to Tous and asked him to return. Tous replied, my sovereign, I swore that I would never turn my back on you and I am going to keep my promise. He then asked Geev to turn back. But Geev replied that he would obey him if he were still the Shah, but seeing that he had abdicated, he would do as he wished. Seeing that further argument would be fruitless, K'Khosro urged Behzad to follow the path to Sepeed-kooh and soon the group of riders were enveloped in fog. Not long afterward, snow began to fall and in the whiteout the riders neither saw the path ahead nor left a track that could be followed and they were never heard of again.

Glossary

Creatures/People

Aashkesh | A warrior from Zabolestan. He drove the caravan from Touran to Iran rescuing Bijan and Manijeh.

Aaz | Embodiment of unsatiable greed. Zurvan made Aaz from their own element and Ahriman's body. Zurvan then gifted Aaz to Ahriman.

Afrasiab | Ruler of Touran. Slayer of Shah Nowzar and Siavosh among many others. The key antagonist in this and many other sagas in the Shahnameh.

Ahriman | Came into existence because Zurvan doubted the desirability of a world created to worship them.

Aspanoo | Amazon warrior who fought alongside Tajaav the keeper of Touran to the West. K'Khosro was infatuated with her, sight unseen, but could not put his own desire above her freedom.

Bahram	Son of Gudarz and Geev's younger brother.
Barsam	A green branch with the power to aid in creation of new beings. It was given to Hormoz by Zurvan to help him in creating the world.
Belashan	Afrasiab's favourite pahlevan and commander of the army sent to repel the invading forces from Iran.
Bijan	Geev's son and a brave pahlevan as well as lover of Manijeh.
Brahma	The Hindu god of creation within the trinity of supreme divinity including Vishnu and Shiva.
Book of destiny	A journal where Zurvan has recorded every event in the life of every being.
Chehra	married to Nozeh and former landowners in Nimrooz in Sistan. They fled to the foothills of Ghalla in northern Touran and lived as shepherdess and shepherd and were foster-parents to K'Khosro from infancy to age thirteen.

Deev	Created by Ahriman, evil creatures that resemble the lovechild of ogres and demons.
Eghrireth	Afrasiab's brother and victim of fratricide by Afrasiab.
Ensan	A pious man sent to the battleground between Hormoz and Ahriman when the latter was about to win. He lived for thirty years and was incorruptible by Ahriman and his demons. In frustration, Ahriman killed him. As he fell, a drop of his seed fell to the ground where a rhubarb grew. Two stalks of this rhubarb took the shape of Mashy & Mashyaneh – the first man and woman.
Faramarz	Rostam's son and a brave pahlevan.
Fariborz	Younger son of Shah K'Kavoos and brother of Siavosh.
Farigees	Daughter of Afrasiab, wife of Siavosh and mother to K'Khosro.
Farr-e-izadi	Being anointed by Zurvan as Shah of Iran. A gift that included extra-

ordinary powers including the ability to see into the future.

Fereydoun
Grandson of Jamshid; ruler of Iran for 500 years; he brought peace and prosperity after the ruinous reign of Zahhaak.

Forood
Half-brother to K'Khosro, son of Siavosh & Jarireh – daughter of Piran.

Garsivaz
Brother of Afrasiab, he took pleasure in beheading Siavosh and many others.

Geev
Son of Gudarz, a giant of a man and an ardent knight. His seven-year quest led to finding K'Khosro in the care of Chehra and Nozeh.

Golbaad
Commander of the cavalry regiment sent by Piran to kill Farigees and Geev and bring back K'Khosro as they attempted to flee from Siavosh-Gerd to Iran.

Golshahr
Piran's wife and confidant.

Gorgin
Renowned pahlevan who accompanied Bijan to Aavaan and

later brought back news of Bijan's capture by Afrasiab.

Gostaham	Son of Shah Nowzar and younger brother of Tous.
Goshtasb	Son of Lohrasb and named as crown prince by K'Khosro.
Gudarz	Ruler of Espahan and father of Geev. Soroush told Gudarz in a dream that the son of Siavosh would be the saviour of Iran. This is how he commissioned his son, Geev, to search for the unknown princeling.
Hoom	The hermit who discovers Afrasiab's lair.
Hormoz	Born of Zurvan who wished to have a world of worshippers, but did not wish to engage in the details of creation. The gestation of Hormoz within Zurvan is said to have taken 1000 years. Hormoz was expected to be Zurvan's first born and to create a world of good creatures and rule over them.
Humaan	Piran's brother; vanquished by Bijan.

Hushang	Shah of Iran, grandson of Kyomars and son of Siamak. A wise ruler who brought peace and prosperity to Iran over his forty-year rule.
Jamshid	Fourth ruler of the Pishdadian dynasty, ruled for over 300 years bringing prosperity, many inventions and longer life expectancy to all. His success led him to believe he was a deity. But the *farr-e-izadi* abandoned him and over-consumption and overpopulation led to famine and pestilence and the collapse of the civilization he had laboured to build.
Jarireh	Daughter of Piran, wife of Siavosh and mother of Forood. A sage who took refuge from Afrasiab with her son but killed herself after Forood was killed.
Mashy & Mashyaneh	They emerged from the rhubarb plant which grew from Ensan's seed. Two stalks became the first man and woman. They were approached by Hormoz and Ahriman who both claimed they had created the world.

Eventually Ahriman corrupted them by making them eat the flesh of animals. After fifty years, they grew interested in one another and their union led to Mashyneh giving birth to twins – a boy and a girl. They ate the twins. Hormoz admonished this act. They then gave birth to six more pairs of boys and girls and all humans are progeny of these seven couples.

K'Kavoos   Shah of Iran who grew insecure and suspicious of all. Farr-e-Izadi parted ways with him and he became a very unpopular ruler. He fathered Siavosh and Fariborz.

K'Khosro   Son of Saivosh and Farigees. Raised by foster parents Nozeh and Chehra from infancy to age thirteen.

Lohrasp   K'Khosro's successor and great grandson of Hushang.

Manijeh   Daughter of Afrasiab and sister to Farigees, fell in love with Bijan and was disowned by her father. She helped Rostam find and rescue Bijan.

Manuchehr	Eighth ruler of the Pishdadian dynasty; father of Nowzar.
Mehrab	Ruler of Kabolestan, son of Zahhaak and father of Rudabeh.
Nakhar	A pahlevan who rode with Forood.
Nastahan	Another of Piran's brothers who died in combat with Bijan.
Nowzar	Shah of Iran, from the Pishdadian dynasty; killed by Afrasiab.
Nozeh	Foster-father to K'Khosro, a landowner who fled with his wife Chehra to the foothills of Ghalla and lived a simple life as a shepherd.
Pashang Sheedeh	Afrasiab's son who was killed by K'Khosro in combat.
Piran	Renowned Commander-in-chief of Touran. Father of Jarireh.
Rakhsh	Rostam's horse.
Rehham	A pahlevan in Tous' army. He lay in ambush with Bijan and injured Forood.
Rieve	A pahlevan and Tous' son-in-law.

Rostam	The greatest pahlevan Iran has ever known. Son of Zaal and Governor of Zabolestan. His side was always victorious in war.
Rudabeh	Daughter of Mehrab, princess of Kabolestan and wife of Zaal.
Saam	Iran's Pahlevan during the reign of Fereydoun, Manuchehr & Nowzar. Father of Zaal.
Shabrang Behzad	The horse of Siavosh and later K'Khosro – literally, black thoroughbred. (Note: heroic horses never die in the Shahnameh. Perhaps their names are passed on through time.)
Siavosh	Son of K'Kavoos, crown prince of Iran. Husband of Farigees and father of K'Khosro.
Simorgh	A mythical bird living in Alborz kooh. Simorgh raised Zaal. (Note: should be credited with the invention of the Cesarean section.)
Soroush	A messenger from the creator.

Sudabeh	Princess of Hamavaran, wife of K'Kavoos. She falsely accused Siavosh of trying to seduce her, forcing him to trial by fire to prove his innocence.
Tajaav	Afrasiab's son-in-law, a renowned pahlevan and commander of the regiment stationed to protect the western approach to the capital of Touran.
Tous	A prince and Son of Shah Nowzar. Carrier of the Golden Boot and Commander-in-chief of Iran's military forces.
Tur	Second son of Fereydoun.
Varuna	Hindu god of fate, sky, oceans and water.
Vaay	In Zurvanism, the angel of wind, war and justice. He binds the hands and feet of the dead to prevent them from succumbing to temptation and reaching for something they desire.
Zaal	Son of Saam, raised by Simorgh, father of Rostam, husband to Rudabeh. Governor of Zabolestan

and wise philosopher as well as brave pahlevan.

Zahhaak	Son of king Merdas. A narcissist with no morals, he was chosen by Ahriman to sow disorder and chaos. Ahriman, disguised as a sycophant, persuades Zahhaak to kill his father and ascend to the throne. Then, Ahriman, disguised as a cook, introduces him to eating flesh. In return for the new found pleasure, Zahhaak grants the cook a favour, who chooses to kiss the king's shoulders and disappears. Two snakes grow out of Zahhaak's shoulders. Finally, Ahriman, disguised as a physician, declares that the snakes cannot be removed and need to be fed with human brains to prevent them from biting Zahhaak. Zahhaak defeated and succeeded Jamshid. His long reign of terror over Iran was finally ended by Fereydoun.
Zaman	Zurvan, time.
Zarasb	Tous' son.

| Zurvan | An entity infinite in space and time. Having failed to realize their initial intent in bringing about a world of worshippers, they decided to predetermine all outcomes for all creatures which were to follow. |

PLACES

| Aavaan | A hamlet on the border with Touran suffering from being overrun by wild boars. |

| Abar-kooh | The capital of Iran. |

| Alborz-kooh | The home of Simorgh. |

| Aradj | Hoom's hometown, a mixed community of followers of Brahma and Zurvan. |

| Ardebil | A city in north-west Iran and north-east of Abar-kooh where demons had established a fort and harassed the locals. |

Arvand	A mighty river in south-west Iran, miraculously crossed by Fereydoun.
Azar-Goshasp	The oldest and most famous fire temple in north-west Iran.
Balkh	A fort in Touran and near today's Mazar-i-sharif in Afghanistan.
Barda	A region west of the Caspian Sea, well known for its high peak and desolate landscape. It is where Hoom had retreated to as a hermit and Afrasiab escaped to avoid his pursuers.
Damavand	Alborz-kooh.
Derangestan	Where Nimrooz was located. A province also called Sistan.
Espahan	For long periods the largest and most prosperous city in Iran, located in its geographic centre. At the time of the events described herein, it was an important city and province governed by Gudarz.

Ghalla	The region where K'Khosro grew up. Remote and lush, the perfect place for Chehra and Nozeh to escape from conflict.
Hamavan	Encampment where Iranian invading forces fell back after their second defeat by Piran.
Kabolestan	The kingdom east of Iran.
Kalat & Jeram	A region of scenic beauty close to Abar-kooh with natural springs and villages nearby.
Kang	A mighty fort where Afrasiab fled to after losing his battle against K'Khosro east of Jayhoon.
Kharazm	A prosperous province east of Iran.
Jayhoon river	A major river defining the border between Touran and Iran.
Kasseh river	Where the pass towards Touran was piled high with timber to set ablaze and trap the advancing army from Iran.

Mazandaran	The province between the Caspian Sea and the Alborz mountains.
Nimrooz	A town in Derangestan where Chehra and Nozeh had been landowners before fleeing to Ghalla.
Sepeed-kooh	Mountain north-east of Abar-kooh, where Forood's fort was located.
Serai	The private quarters of royal ladies, their children and their entourage.
Sheeth Lake	A small lake where Afrasiab fled from Hoom's custody. He re-emerged at hearing his brother's cries of agony.
Siavosh-Gerd	Province given to Siavosh and Farigees to rule. Their hard work brought unprecedented prosperity and security there.
Sogdia	The region between Amu Darya and Syr Darya.

Touran	A country to the east of Iran roughly where we call Turkmenistan in modern maps.
Tappeh-Sukhteh	The remaining mound of ashes near Abar-kooh where Siavosh rode through fire to prove his fealty and innocence to K'Kavoos.
Zabol	Capital of Zabolestan and home to Saam, Zaal and Rostam.
Zabolestan	In southeastern Iran, roughly Sistan province of Iran in modern maps.
Zam	In northeast Iran, Zam is the closest Iranian town to the border with Touran.
Zayande-rood	A magnificent, meandering river flowing adjacent to Espahan in central Iran.

Acknowledgements

We are enormously indebted to feedback from Soheila Hagighat, Zahra and Francis Dowlatabadi. Francis gave invaluable advice on how to structure the book. Zahra was a tireless editor whose careful reading led to many improvements and better flow of the narrative. Finally, Soheila provided the delightful rendering of K'Khosro on the horns of the dilemma between fatalism and free will.

About the Author and Translator

Hushang Dowlatabadi is a retired physician and active author with an enduring interest in human and animal behaviour. This is his seventh novel, all in Persian. He has also translated Conrad Lorenz's "On Aggression" into Persian. He lives and works in Tehran, Iran.

Hadi Dowlatabadi is a retired physicist who focuses on uncertainties in science and labile social norms. He employs this perspective in trying to improve policies in environmental protection and public health. He lives and works in Vancouver, Canada.

Asemana Books

Devoted to Publishing Diasporic, Underrepresented and Progressive Literature on the Middle East.

✉ Email: Asemanabooks@gmail.com

🌐 Webpage: asemanabooks.ca

Scholarly and Academic Research

- *Tanglusha of a Thousand Images: Essays on Culture and Literature* – Reza Farokhfal – 2024

- *Language, People, and Society: Iranian Minority Languages and Literary Traditions* – Edited by Amir Kalan, Mahdi Ganjavi, Anisa Jafari, Lale Javanshir – 2024

- *Music on the Borderland: Remembering and Chronicling the 1979 Revolution's Shadow on Iranian Music* – Keyan Emami – 2024

- *Implications of Class Analysis in Capitalist Imperialism* – Mohammad Hajinia and Shahrzad Mojab – 2024

- *Dark Night and Phoenixes of the Ashes: Nima Yushij's Poetry from 1932–1942* – Ramin Ahmadi – 2024

- *Whispers of Oasis: Likoo's Poetic Mirage* – Mahdi Ganjavi, Amin Fatemi, Mansour Alimoradi – 2024

- *Hafez and Irony* – Reza Farokhfal – 2024

- *Kurdish Women at the Core of the Historical Contradictions on Feminism and Nationalism* – Shahrzad Mojab – 2023

- *The Peasant Uprising of Mukriyan 1952–1953: Consulate Documents, Diplomatic Correspondence, and the Press Coverage* – Amir Hassanpour – 2022

Critical Edition

- *The History of Changes in Iran* – Mirza Agha Khan Kermani, edited by M. Rezaei Tazik – 2024
- *Rostam in the Twenty-Second Century* – Abdulhussain San'atizadeh Kermani, edited by Mahdi Ganjavi and M. Mansouri – 2017

Poetry

- *Shape of Extinction* – Poetry of Bijan Jalali, Translated by Adeeba Shahid Talukder and Aria Fani - 2025
- *One Hundred Nights of Yearning* – Mansour Noorbakhsh – 2025
- *Songs of Barbad* – Amir Hakimi – 2024
- *With My Shadows, I Created Myself* – Hadi Ebrahimi Roudbaraki - 2024
- *Citizens of September* – Saeid Rezadoust - 2024
- *Wonder of Memory* – Amir Hakimi – 2023
- *Galaxy Has No Memory of the Sunset* – Mahdi Ganjavi – 2023
- *Strangers Who Live in Me* – Mahdi Ganjavi – 2021
- *Exiled to the Rocky* – Ali Fatolahi – 2018

Fiction & Plays

- *Escape from the Girl's Complex* _ Mahbobe Mousavi – 2025
- *Yousef, Joseph, Guiseppe* – Ali Foumani - 2025
- *An Iranian Odyssey* – Rana Soleimani – 2025
- *Lead to Evil* – Javad Alavi – 2025
- *We Are Drunk and Broken, and No One Is Witnessing Us* – Mahdi Ganjavi – 2025
- *Someone Had Died in Front of Our House* – Akbar Falahzadeh – 2024
- *Zinat* – Vahid Zarrabi Nasab – 2024
- *Siberian Crane* – Ali Foumani - 2024
- *Elephants Reached the Plain* – Kaveh Oveisi - 2024
- *Textual Mosaic* – Marzieh Sotoudeh – 2024
- *Expectations of a Dream* – Mahdi Ganjavi – 2020

Asemana Books is devoted to publishing diasporic,
underrepresented, and progressive literature on the Middle East.

asemanabooks.ca

ASEMANA
BOOKS

www.ingramcontent.com/pod-product-compliance
Lightning Source LLC
Chambersburg PA
CBHW030634030726
47497CB00006B/1784